WRONGFUL
DEATH

WRONGFUL DEATH

DANIEL MCLINDEN

ARPress
45 Dan Road Suite 15
Canton MA 02021

Hotline: 1(800) 220-7660
Fax: 1(855) 752-6001

Ordering Information:
Quantity sales. Special discounts are available on quantity purchases by corporations, associations, and others. For details, contact the publisher at the address above.

Printed in the United States of America.

ISBN-13:   Paperback   979-8-89676-614-8
                  eBook   979-8-89676-615-5

Library of Congress Control Number: 2021916635

HOLLYWOOD. Harry opened his eyes none too soon. A garbage truck's low gear groaned, brakes squealed, and deafening hydraulics echoed throughout the narrow tree-lined street where he lived.

He threw on jeans, flew out the back door, grabbed a battered 20-gallon metal can near the garage and dashed barefoot down a sun-splashed driveway. Two loose gravel stones embedded into his heel and had him hopping to the finish.

The garbage man took the can out of Harry's hand and upended its contents into the bin. Harry brushed the stones from his foot.

A young woman emerged from the passenger side of a Mercedes sports car, blocked-in behind the garbage truck. She wore black heels and a blue-grey stewardess uniform. The purse, dangling from her shoulder, whooshed by Harry.

He watched her go clicking and clacking to the front stoop of the apartment building next door. She fumbled for keys and glanced back at him. The sun was on her. She had dark glistening hair and actress looks.

Harry gave her a friendly nod. But she just looked away. Deflated, he marched the empty can up the driveway.

Harry stepped through the back door of his house to a tail-wagging German Shepard named Boomer. Boomer bounded to the far corner of the kitchen and stood guard over an empty dog bowl. Harry filled it with Pedigree morsels and chopped chicken.

A moment later, Boomer and Harry heard a woman's bloodcurdling scream. It came from a top-floor apartment next door. Harry stepped out back. He looked up and listened for another scream. None came.

Concerned, Harry walked to the front of the apartment building. It was quiet there. He pressed buttons on the resident directory until he got buzzed in. He took the stairs to the top floor and walked down a long hallway. The air was dank and musty. He heard faint sounds from TVs and radios, some music, but no quarrels or screams. He wondered why there was no commotion. He thought about knocking on every door. But after looking at the aging building with its creaking floors and frayed carpets he chalked the scream up to a rodent.

Going back to his house, he stopped to pick up the LA Times from the walkway. The front page had a large color photo of a years' younger Elvis on it, framed in black and underscored with "1935 – 1977."

Stunned, Harry shuffled to the porch and opened the front door to the two-bedroom bungalow. Behind him now, and running toward him from the apartment building, was the stewardess.

"Please. Please. Can I come in?"

He nodded to her. She brushed past him into the living room. Fear blanketed her face. Boomer greeted her -- snout to crotch. Harry yanked Boomer back by the collar.

"I need to hide."

"What's wrong?"

"Someone's after me."

"Who."

"I can't tell you."

"I'll call the police."

"Don't. He'll leave."

"How do you know?"

"He will."

She went to the front window at the side of the house and kept her eye on the entrance to the apartment building. Harry kept one eye on her and one on the entrance. She had sable-colored eyes, high cheek bones, flaring nostrils, and an expressive mouth.

She and Harry stood there like statues. Not a word between them. Even Boomer stood immobile but poised to pounce.

A blonde-haired man in a leather jacket and jeans walked hurriedly from the apartment building toward the end of the block.

"Is that him?" Harry asked.

The stewardess nodded.

"I've got to get back to my apartment."

"Are you sure?"

"Yes."

"Would you like me to go with you?"

"No. I'm OK."

"Shouldn't you call the police?"

"I will."

"What's your name?"

She thought about answering.

"Cleo."

Harry widened his eyes and tilted his head.

"Cleo Whelan. Look. I'm sure you've got work. I'll call the police."

"Are you sure?"

"Yes. I can do it."

"By the way, my name is Harry McHugh."

HARRY WENT TO WORK, thinking he'd get a courthouse run, where he could swing by his neighborhood on the way back from downtown, and check in on Cleo.

But wouldn't you know it. The hottest day of the year, and at noon he got a motion-filing in the Indio Superior Court about three hours away, past Palm Springs, in the desert. It would take him the whole rest of the day.

Becky, the receptionist, steered the trip to Harry. She had a crush on him. It was a dream run. Crank on the radio, sit back and collect mileage money every minute of the trip.

The Mazda's air conditioning was out. Harry drove with the windows down. Ordinarily, he'd get to Indio and step from the car into a furnace. This time no such shock. The shock came when he walked into the courthouse. It was fifty degrees cooler.

He had to get back to the office with the conformed copies of the motion he'd filed. That meant braving rush hour traffic the last several miles.

It was after 6 o'clock when he stepped off the elevator on the 17th floor. A majority of the attorneys and much of the staff were still there, billing and slaving away. Becky's back was turned to him. She was straightening her station when Harry, walking by, rapped his knuckles on her counter.

"Hi, Beck. I'm putting this on Liliana's chair."

"OK. See me before you leave."

Becky had a new messenger slip for him, to pick up Perrier at Smart & Final on his way in the next day.

"Oh. And go see Rachel when you get in tomorrow. She has a research assignment for you."

"Thanks, Becky," he said, heading to the elevators.

Her eyes remained fixed on him through the glass entryway. Becky was 20, from Calabasas, a well-heeled hilly nabe inland from Malibu. She was smart in a lot of ways: guile and cunning from mom, a doctor's wife; more brains, from dad, a cancer specialist. She knew herself and her assets. She was chomping at the bit to use them on Harry.

BACK HOME, HARRY fed Boomer, leashed him up, and started his walk by detouring to the apartment building next door. Harry looked for "WHELAN" on the directory to buzz Cleo. Not there. He pressed "Manager."

"Yes?" came over the intercom.

"I've got a delivery for Ms. Whelan."

"Ms. Who?"

"Whelan."

"Sorry. No one here by that name."

"OK."

It wasn't the first time a woman had given Harry a wrong name or phone number. He narrowed his search to the top floor where the scream came from. And narrowed it further to female occupants only. There were no Cleos listed. He started pressing numbers to sneak in. Someone buzzed him in. He went in with Boomer at his side, sniffing all the way.

He knocked on the doors of the numbers he'd narrowed his search to. The doors cracked inward the length of their chain locks. None of the faces he saw was Cleo's. The apartment with no answer was rented to a Brigette Whitecloud.

After the walk, Harry looked up at Brigette Whitecloud's apartment windows. They were dark.

He called information. No Cleo Whelan listed. Brigette Whitecloud was. He called. No answer.

AT WORK NEXT DAY, Rachel Rabin gave Harry five depositions to summarize for an upcoming trial. She needed them by Monday. They would take him all weekend to do. He had a knack for distilling depositions into short spurts of plain English.

Rachel would only use Harry, no other paralegals, for her paralegal work.

OVER THE WEEKEND Harry kept looking for any sign of life in Brigette's place but there was none, neither shadows nor lights. Harry saw a neighbor going into the apartment building.

"Excuse me," he said, do you know Brigette upstairs in 407?"

"No. Sorry."

Harry was used to serving summonses and complaints on people. He snuck in again and went back to the fourth floor. He knocked on the apartment door of the girl he found most friendly on his last attempt.

"Hi, I'm back, without my dog this time."

"Hi."

"Do you know Brigette in 407?"

"Yes."

"Have you seen her lately?"

"No."

"If you see her will you tell her Jimmy stopped by?"

"Sure."

"Oh. Is she still flying?"

"Flying?"

"Still a stewardess?"

"I thought she was a secretary?"

"Oh yeah. Stupid me. Where was it she worked?"

"Prudential."

"Yeah. That's it. Remember, tell her Jimmy stopped by?"

"Sure."

"Thanks."

"And what's your name?"

"Cindy."

"Thanks, Cindy. By the way is there any stewardess in the building?"

"Not that I know of."

"OK. Thanks again."

Harry thought he'd struck out. Brigette was a secretary. Cleo was a stewardess.

THE NEXT EVENING Harry sat outside on the porch with Boomer. His house would not let go of the day's heat and poor Boomer could use the fresh air. Harry had the radio on a low volume. He was listening to the Dodger game. Jerry Doggett was announcing the middle innings. The Dodgers led the Padres 4 to 2. Davey Lopes was up with two outs, bases empty.

Harry saw a woman walking up the steps of the apartment building next door. She looked like Cleo. Harry shot up and Boomer pulled the wrought iron table he was tethered to across the porch.

"Cleo? Cleo?" Harry called after the woman.

She was pressing a button to get in. She turned to Harry and looked at him.

"I'm sorry." Harry added. "I thought you were someone else."

"That's OK," the woman said.

"Oh. Excuse me, do you know Brigette?"

"I was just buzzing her."

"I haven't seen her for over a week," Harry said.

The woman nodded.

"I live next door," Harry said, trying to keep the conversation going, but immediately thinking how lame his statement must have sounded considering where he was standing.

I never would have guessed, the woman thought to herself.

"She's not answering."

"Wait a sec," Harry said, "I'll see if any lights are on in her apartment."

Harry hopped over the porch and went up the driveway. He returned shaking his head. She had followed him to the corner of the building.

"No lights."

"OK."

"Are you worried about her?"

"A little."

"Say I don't mean to sound forward, but would you like a coffee or something to drink?"

She found Harry attractive even with the lame comment, or maybe because of it.

"OK. Sure."

Harry led her to the porch. She had on salmon shorts, a white crop top, and tan sandals. Boomer leaned into her for a pat on the head.

"He's never that friendly."

"I love dogs."

"Do you live around here?"

"On Waring near Poinsettia."

"Neighbors."

"Mm-hmm."

Once inside, Harry said, "Have a seat." Continuing to the kitchen, he added, "Coffee or Coke?"

"Coke. A real one if you have it."

"That's all I got. Be careful with him. He can get rough."

Harry dropped a couple ice cubes into two glasses, poured the Coke into them, and watched it fizz to the top.

She had enticed Boomer onto his back and was rubbing his belly. Harry hurried the glass into her hand to prevent an awkward moment with a big pink Boomer boner in it.

"His name is Boomer."

"What a sweetheart." Looking about, she added, "Nice place."

"A friend of mine found it. A woman he worked with got it in a divorce and rented it to me to cover her alimony."

"You're paying alimony?"

She was teasing him. He could tell.

"Say, what's your name?"

"Toby Maize. Yours?"

"Harry McHugh."

"How do you know Brigette?"

"Look. I don't want to alarm you. But she came over last Wednesday morning to hide from a blonde guy who was after her. She told me she was going to call the police."

"What?"

"I know. It was the first time I'd seen her. And look. I really don't want to alarm you, but I'm not sure the woman who came over was actually Brigette."

"What?"

"Here's the deal. The woman who came over said she was Cleo. I thought she lived on the 4th floor next door. When I went to see if she was OK and had contacted the police like she said she would, there was no Cleo, only Brigette. But Brigette wasn't home and hasn't been for a week. Confusing, I know. Say does Brigette have black hair and black eyes, a blonde boyfriend?"

"She does. 'Cleo' is the name she gives out when guys are hitting on her and she doesn't want them to know who she really is."

"So, she was Brigette."

"I think so. But I can't understand why she wouldn't have told you her real name, Harry."

"You mean I'm real-name-worthy?"

"Take it from Mary."

Harry laughed.

"So, is it Toby Maize or Mary Maize?"

"Toby."

"Another thing. Is she a stewardess or secretary?"

"Secretary."

"Good."

"Why? Do you have something against stewardesses?"

"No. Do you think we should report her missing to the police?"

"I think so."

"Who's the blonde guy?"

"Lead singer from Offramp. Arnold Jensen."

"She's dating him?"

"Long story. I had the manager of Offramp on a flight and he invited all the stewardesses to a recording session at Capitol Records."

"You're a stewardess?"

"Yes."

"Good!"

Toby rolled her eyes at him.

"When I first saw her last Thursday, she was in a stewardess uniform."

"You sure?"

"Yes."

"That's strange."

"So, go on."

"Brigette was there. At the recording session. When the session broke up, the other stewardesses corralled the musicians, fine with me, but it put Brigette in a snit.

"We both got on the elevator together and started talking about the music. I'd pressed street level and she'd pressed P-1. When we got to street level, she asked me if I needed a ride. I told her I was walking home, it wasn't far, and she said she'd give me a lift.

"She had something going with the lead singer and was mad he got wrapped up with the stewardesses. She told me he was kinky for uniforms.

"After that, I bumped into her a couple times in the neighborhood. We started doing things together."

"Who does she work for?"

"She's a secretary for Prudential."

"He's kinky for uniforms?"

"That's what she said. I took it like a throwaway comment. A dig. She was mad at him. And her competition that morning were stewardesses. But now, maybe the comment meant more than I thought. Like it was literally true. Maybe it explains why she was wearing a uniform last week. I wonder if she's still working or hiding out. I wonder if she's OK."

"Look. I can go to Prudential and see if she's there. I'd rather do that, than call the cops for no good reason. I can go tomorrow."

"Will you do that, Harry?"

"Sure."

"And let me know?"

"Mm-hmm. Say, is Brigette from LA?"

"No. She's from Ogallala, Nebraska."

"Where are you from?"

"Washington State, a very small town, Elma."

"More Coke or some chips?"

"No, thanks. I gotta go now."

"I'll walk you if you like."

"That'd be great."

The walk was pleasant. She asked Harry what he did. Harry told her he worked for a law firm. He was a messenger and paralegal, went to law school at night. They talked about LA and tried not to step on the enormous cockroaches that would come out on hot nights like that one. The bugs, scurrying across the sidewalks, baffled Boomer.

HARRY HAD TO hand-deliver last minute discovery responses to an opposing attorney's office in mid-Wilshire, across from the Prudential Building.

Before leaving for the run, Harry typed an address on a Schwartz & Weiss envelope: "Ms. Brigette Whitecloud,

PRUDENTIAL INSURANCE COMPANY, 5757 Wilshire Boulevard, Los Angeles, California 90036."

Harry walked into the Prudential Building and stopped at the information desk in front of the elevator well. He told the guard he had a letter for Ms. Whitecloud but did not know her floor. The guard reached over the counter and pulled out a clipboard. Standing sideways to Harry, he flipped to the end of several pages of names.

"Not here."

Harry, spying the names, pointed to "Whitecloud." "Isn't that her?"

"She's crossed out." The guard turned the board to Harry so he could see for himself.

"No longer here."

"Oh. Right."

Harry saw numbers he took for a phone extension and "14th Floor" next to the name.

At five o'clock Harry went up to the 14th Floor and told the receptionist he had a letter for Brigette Whitecloud. The receptionist's cheerful smile went away.

"I'm sorry. She no longer works here."

"Oh. Do you have a forwarding address?"

"No."

"Do you know where she's working now?"

"No."

"Did you know her?"

"Yes."

"Look. This isn't a summons or complaint. Nothing bad."

"But I can't help you."

"OK. Is there anyone here I could talk to?"

"Not really."

She looked in the direction of a minor commotion. It was a group of girls leaving for the night. She looked back at Harry, raised her eyebrows and leaned her head toward them.

"The girl in lavender," she whispered.

"Thanks. Her name?"

"Monica."

Harry got on an elevator with seven women. He listened to their post-work small talk and smiled each time they laughed.

When the door opened on the bottom floor, he sidled up to Monica.

"Excuse me, Monica?"

"Yes?"

"I'm sorry to bother you, but I have a letter here for Brigette Whitecloud." He held it up.

"I'm sorry. I haven't seen her."

"Do you know what happened to her."

"No. She just quit. I tried to call her, but no answer. You know. I think I've told you too much already."

"Do me a favor. No. Never mind. Look. If I find her, I'll call you."

"OK."

"What's your number?"

"(213) 531-1182."

Harry took a pen from his pocket and scribbled the number on the envelope.

Harry wanted her to commit to calling him if she heard anything but was satisfied to get her number. He could always call her and pump her for more information.

Going to Prudential landed on Harry like a ton of bricks. Brigette Whitecloud was dead or missing or both. And he was running around like an amateur sleuth. He went from the Prudential Building straight to the Hollywood Police Station.

Harry was seated, waiting for an interview. A handsome, young, black man, sharply dressed in a tan suit, pale yellow shirt and cranberry tie walked toward Harry and asked him if he needed help. Harry told him he needed to talk to a detective.

"I'm Detective Fields. Come on back to my desk."

Harry ended up telling Detective Fields all the details he recalled. The detective told him he'd get on it.

Harry called Toby to tell her the police were going to look for Brigette.

The next evening there was a knock on Harry's door. It was Detective Fields.

"Mr. McHugh would you like to come with me to the apartment next door and see if there's anything there you saw on Ms. Whitecloud?"

"Sure. Have you seen the apartment?"

"Yes. Just now."

Harry didn't see the stewardess uniform or the purse. He thought the black heels in the closet were the ones she wore.

Detective Fields told Harry he had arranged with the apartment manager for forensics to come in the following day, and after that, the apartment could be re-let. For now, it was a missing-person case.

ON A HOT, MUGGY Saturday night a few days later, Harry was trying to study for summer-session finals. The Dodger game was on the radio, the windows were open, and there was a constant ruckus coming from the Chabad House across the street.

The former owner of the house, Dora Silverstein, had been a concert pianist. When she died, she left the property to the Jewish charity. It was used for a rehab and halfway house that catered to short-term residents, mostly teenagers, with drug and other issues.

That summer about a dozen pregnant, unmarried teenagers from New York came out for several weeks and were crammed together into the three-bedroom house.

They'd whistle at Harry from their porch whenever he'd go in or come out the front door.

And nearly every weekend night, they'd yak on and on, yelling and screaming, laughing, and having an uproarious time of it. The noise drove Harry from the front room to the back of the house to study. He knew they'd go on all night.

Next morning, Harry grabbed his baseball glove and a ball and went out the front door with Boomer. The Chabad girls were still asleep. Harry's neighbor Gail was standing in front of her house, watering flowers. Harry had heard Gail yelling at the Chabad girls to shut up the night before, nearly every hour on the hour. After she yelled, it would go quiet for a minute or two, then they'd start right back up.

A year back, when Gail was promoted at Paramount in the costume department, she bought the place next to Harry and moved in with her partner, Pepper, and Pepper's son, Sean. Harry had come over to welcome them to the neighborhood, and ended up helping them move in.

"Morning, Gail."

"Hi, Harry."

"I heard you yelling at our neighbors last night. What time did the racket stop?"

"1:17 a.m."

"That's early for them on a Saturday night. How do you know the exact time?"

"Because I looked at the clock in the kitchen at 1:16, walked out the back door and across the street with the .357 Magnum, I got from the prop department, and waved it at them. They huddled-up and screamed on the front porch, pushing and shoving each other to get away from me, and retreat into the house through the front door. I told them if I heard one more peep out of them, I'd blow their fuckin' heads off."

Harry roared.

"Post-script, Harry. One of them went into labor. I delivered it myself. They named her Gail, broke with their orthodox upbringing, and appointed me godmother. All thanks to the Second Amendment, my familiarity with vaginas, and mostly, the first aid training I got from the studio.

"You should have seen it. Pepper came over and I got her to snip the umbilical cord. Other than that, Pepper was Butterfly McQueen. Not only is Pepper the spitting image of Prissy, but just like Prissy, Pepper don't know nothin' 'bout birthin' babies. She had an epidural with Sean and didn't pay a whole lot of attention to what was going on."

Harry kept laughing.

"Is Sean home?"

"Yeah."

"I told him I'd play catch."

"Here, Harry, hold the hose. I'll get him."

HARRY FOUND a business card taped to the front door. It was from Detective Fields with a note on it to call him.

"The whole place had been wiped clean," Detective Fields began, "we picked up a few prints of hers, some from the apartment manager, but no one else, not even a partial."

"What do you make of it?"

"With any wiping like that, foul play's possible. I'll keep you posted."

FALL SEMESTER meant Criminal Procedure, Family Law, and Wills and Trusts for Harry. He had a lot on his plate with work, studies, the Dodger pennant drive and getting Rachel ready for trial. He stopped thinking about Cleo, but not about Toby.

A bunch of secretaries invited him to a party in the Valley. There was going to be a hot tub there. "Don't bring your trunks!" they told him. Becky planned to make her move.

Harry was torn. He needed every minute of the weekend for studying. He toyed with the idea of going to the party or not.

He knew if he went, he'd have to contend with two or three secretaries hellbent on nailing him. He chickened out.

On Monday morning the office was abuzz with the highs and lows of the weekend. The secretaries banded against Harry when he showed up at work. He didn't even try making an excuse for why he hadn't gone to the party. When he got his first run of the day, Becky whispered to him on his way out, that Barbara had stripped for the hot tub.

"Now are you sorry you didn't go, Harry?"

HARRY'S STUDY GROUP met every other week on Sunday afternoons at his house. Carol, Penny and Miguel would come over with pizza and salad.

They tried to make sense of all the new concepts they were stuffing their brains with, to put plain meaning to it all. Harry and Miguel were less vocal than the girls, and often felt, listening to them, only along for the ride.

Penny was divorced, not working, with all the time in the world to study; Carol, also single, was a secretary to a movie producer; Miguel had a trucking company, four box trucks, in East LA; and, Harry had his foot in the door at Schwartz & Weiss.

Study group was always a good time. The best part of law school. They'd argue the facts and argue the law. They'd theorize how courts reached outcomes in cases, what factors were key, what could have made a difference, and what was missing.

Harry came to think Carol had the best legal mind of the group. Her explanations were spot-on. Miguel had a flair for looking at facts and reaching correct conclusions, but without being able to explain how he got there. Penny was in knots over every detail. Harry was none of those things.

Harry remembered everything. He wasn't an abstract thinker or intuitive when it came to how courts dealt with the cases before them. He'd remember what happened in each case he read.

The four night-students made a diverse group. Each one in their own way strengthened the others.

When they went off track, Penny would reel them back, unless it was her, talking about her daughter. Penny'd groan if Miguel brought up his favorite subject, "The Godfather" films. She'd cut Carol a little slack when she'd go on about the troubles her twin sister was having with men. Penny had no beef with Harry. He stuck to the law, and otherwise was content to listen.

But down deep Penny obsessed whether Harry was gay or not with his James-Dean looks. He never talked about women and she knew he spent every weekend studying.

At first, she tried to lure him in. Her failure confirmed Harry's gayness to her. Her belief was reinforced when Carol's overtures to Harry also fell short. Carol thought Penny was nuts. And Miguel knew Harry wasn't gay, because Miguel was.

DETECTIVE FIELDS drove up Laurel Canyon Boulevard and pulled into the driveway of a hillside home, hidden behind a solid redwood fence and a privacy gate on rails. He buzzed at the gate and said he was Detective Fields, Los Angeles Police Department, for Arnold Jensen.

"What's this about?" came the reply.

"Are you Mr. Jensen?"

"Yes."

"I need to ask you a few questions about Brigette Whitecloud."

Surprisingly, without much hesitation, Jensen replied, "Do you have a warrant?"

"No."

"Stay there."

After a few minutes Arnold Jensen came through the door in the fence to the left of the gate. He was thin with long blonde hair. He wore jeans and a dark-green sweatshirt. No smile, no extended hand, or any type of greeting. He started right in with a rehearsed response.

"My lawyer said it was OK to talk to you. She was a groupie. I haven't seen her for months. I couldn't tell you where she lives or where she's from."

"Do you know where she worked?"

"No."

"Was she a stewardess?"

"I don't know."

"Where'd you meet her?"

"Backstage at a concert."

"When?"

"About a year ago."

"Ever take her out?"

"What d'ya mean?

"To dinner. A movie. Anything like that?"

"No."

"Go anywhere with her?"

"I'd take her to a motel."

"Which one?"

"The ones along Sunset."

"Ever bring her here?"

"No."

"Ever bring her to a recording session?"

"I don't think so."

"Capitol Records?"

"That's where I record."

"Ever hear she went missing?"

"No."

"Ever lend her your car?"

"No."

"Did she ever take your car?"

"She borrowed it after a recording session once."

"She borrowed it?"

"Yes. That's what I just said."

"And you also said before that, that you never lent it to her."

"Look. I got a gig at the Troubadour and I'm running late."

"OK. Here's my card. Please give me a call if you hear from her, or anything about her."

Jensen took the card.

A FEW DAYS LATER, Detective Fields saw Arnold Jensen at the Troubadour and told Jensen he was finishing his investigation by conducting short interviews with the other bandmembers. He said he did not want to track them down at home, or call them into the station, and could probably wrap things up in about 20 minutes. Jensen didn't argue.

Each bandmember admitted seeing Brigette backstage a few times. She'd go off with Arnie. She was at an all-night session at Capitol for last year's album. The bass player had a couple conversations with her. He knew she worked as a secretary, and she was from Nebraska. She had asked him if Arnie had drug problems. He'd told her no, just a fierce temper.

When asked if Arnie ever told him anything about Brigette, the bass player said Arnie told him to give her four Vicodin once. The bass player said she and Arnie'd come back to Arnie's and she was crying and upset. It was last summer. It was the last time he saw her.

The bass player had asked Brigette what'd happened, and she said she could not tell anyone. He asked her if she was afraid of Arnie, and she said no, but he didn't believe her.

Detective Fields asked him what Brigette was wearing when Jensen asked for the Vicodin. A skimpy pirate outfit, but it wasn't Halloween.

"Did Jensen have a thing for costumes?"

"He might," said the bass player. "With all these groupies the norm is full kink across the board. It's an occupational hazard for rockers."

"Would you please ask Mr. Jensen to come in here. Tell him I need to see him before I leave."

"Sure."

Jensen walked into the dressing room where Detective Fields had conducted the bandmember interviews.

"I just wanted to thank you. Good luck with your set tonight."

"Yeah."

"Oh. One more thing. Did you ever tell Bryan to give Brigette four Vicodin?"

"No."

"Did Brigette ever wear a pirate costume with you?"

"No."

"Or a stewardess uniform?"

Jensen shook his head from side to side.

"OK. Thanks."

Jensen seethed before, during and after the performance. He asked Bryan what he had told the cop. Bryan's response to him left out the bad stuff. In truth, Bryan despised Arnie. He liked Brigette.

Detective Fields sent a couple music-loving undercover cops to the Troubadour and had them tail Jensen after his set. He drove straight home. The officers hung around for a few hours, but Jensen never came out.

HARRY MADE IT A POINT after meeting Toby to walk Boomer on Waring Avenue. But he never caught sight of her.

The Dodgers lost the World Series to the Yankees, and it sent Harry into a funk.

Weeks rolled by. The pregnant teenagers went back east. Gail caught up on sleep.

But soon the new residents at the Chabad House were back at it. There was a loud, menacing skinhead ruling the roost over there. He'd hang out on the front porch and harass every passerby. He looked like a Neo-Nazi to Harry, which made no sense, given the environment.

It turned out the skinhead was an ex-Israeli soldier who'd had lice. He did not last long. Literally. A housemate of his, a frail Iranian Jew, the skinhead had kept bullying, went into a fit of rage.

The Iranian Jew grabbed a butcher knife from the kitchen drawer, rushed the skinhead, whose military training almost saved him. The butcher knife ended up plunged deep into the skinhead's gut. And that was just the beginning. Paramedics called to the scene counted seventeen stab wounds.

In the aftermath of it all, the Chabad House's Board of Directors turned to a young Sephardic couple, the Toledanos, to have them move in and raise their family there. *Hallelujah!*

"HEY BOOMER!" A woman yelled as she got out of a car on Waring Avenue. Boomer and Harry stopped in their tracks and swirled around. It was dark, but the silhouette hopping onto the sidewalk was unmistakable.

"Hi, Toby."

"Hey, Harry."

"How have you been?"

"Good."

"How 'bout you?"

"Not bad."

"Any news of Brigette?"

"Nope."

"Wanna come in? Had supper?"

"I'd love to, but I gotta get to class. Rain check?"

"OK. Next time it rains, Harry."

"Come on, Toby. This is Southern California. It could be months."

"I'll do a rain dance."

Harry wanted to ask her if she was Native American. She could see him thinking.

"Spit it out Harry. You're wondering if that kind of dance is in my repertoire."

"Is it?"

"Never needed one. Humptulips never dance for rain. It's all around them."

"That's right. You're from Washington. What tribe did you say?"

"Humptulip."

"What a cool name. Wait a second, Toby. Isn't the purpose of a raincheck to cash it in whenever you please?"

"That's right, Harry."

"How 'bout we go out this Friday?"

"You're on."

———— ❦ ————

HARRY CALLED TOBY after class. "Have you seen "A Chorus Line?"

"No. You're kidding me!"

"I'll pick you up at 6:30. Eight o'clock curtain." Harry left a lot of leeway. Friday night traffic could be brutal.

"Thanks, Harry."

Toby wore a pistachio green dress, ruby pumps, and a rose suede cadet jacket; her hair, in double braids. Harry wore brown tweed slacks, cognac-colored dress shoes, and a black cashmere crewneck sweater over a white dress shirt. The two of them had Bullocks Wilshire, May Company, and the Hollywood Thrift Store to thank for it.

The Shubert Theater sat over two-thousand people. Both Harry and Toby were there for the first time. They soaked in the massive crowd, the décor, the fashion, and the perfume in the air. There was a tangible excitement from the hubbub of the theatergoers and stomach butterflies when the house lights went out.

Toby took Harry's hand during the play.

At intermission in the big lobby Harry saw a familiar face.

"Tailing me?" Harry asked wryly.

"Nice to see you."

"You, too. This is Toby Maize. And this is Detective Fields, LAPD."

"Hello, Toby. This is Ella. And Ella, this is Harry." Helloes and smiles all around. "Ella's mom grew up with Willie Mays."

"Wow," said Harry, "660."

"I'm Maize, M-A-I-Z-E."

"Like Indian corn," detective Fields added.

"I'm half Indian."

"And?" asked Ella.

"Half Norwegian."

"You're gorgeous, girl!" exclaimed Ella.

"Thanks. So are you."

The men raised their eyebrows and glanced askance at each other.

Teddy, except for a camel sport coat, was dressed all in black, shoes, pants and shirt, with the top button of his shirt, buttoned. Toby thought he looked like Sam Cooke.

Ella had on a black midi-dress with sleeves, high neckline and a plunging V-back. Her skin was an alluring espresso. Her hair was braided. She had perfect features, wide beautiful light brown eyes, classic nose and seductive mouth.

The lights flickered off-and-on a couple times.

"Well, nice to meet you."

"You, too. Enjoy the play."

"Isn't it great?" said Ella.

"For sure," said Toby.

It was eleven o'clock when Harry and Toby rolled out of the Century City parking garage onto Olympic Boulevard.

"Where to?" Harry asked.

"What do you think?"

"I don't know."

"Hmm? How does apple pie a la mode and coffee sound?"

"Canter's?"

"Better yet. If you stop at The Boys' Market on Santa Monica beyond Vista, there's a table with today's pies, baked on site on it, half price. But maybe you'd like something else?"

"No. That sounds good."

Toby's place was a small studio, neat as a pin. She flipped on the stereo and put on Wes Montgomery's "Bumpin' on Sunset" -- a mellow jazz LP. She put the coffee on, clicked the gas stove into action and slid the pie onto a baking pan already on one of the racks. She let the ice cream sit out.

They talked about the play and how they ended up in LA. The more they talked the more they were drawn to each other.

It was getting late, the week had caught up to them, the coffee wore off, and they sank closer together on the couch. Toby could not keep her eyes open and Harry was right behind her.

Harry wanted to pop open the sofabed, have Toby flop on one side of it, and pat the other side, to signal him to join her.

But instead, he encircled Toby with his arms, pressed his lips to her cheek, and whispered, "I've got to let Boomer out."

Eyes closed, she whispered back, "Sorry, Harry. You're a few dates too early for that."

"Haah! I meant my dog."

She laughed at herself, got composed, and gave him a sweet parting kiss.

BOOMER WAS SLEEPING behind the back door. When he heard the Mazda, he jumped up and scratched hard at the door until Harry unlocked it.

Next morning Harry called Toby, looking to see her again. She told him her first day off was Wednesday. Harry had class that night.

"How 'bout we talk in a few days?"

"OK, Harry. Sounds good."

Harry broke out the law books, turned on a college football game in the background and started reading criminal procedure and jotting down notes into a college-rule notebook.

Next day his default thought of Toby multiplied. He walked Boomer, played catch with Sean, studied a little, and cleaned the house for the study group.

Miguel arrived first. He came the farthest and satisfied what came to be known as Miguel's maxim: "First to arrive at any event is the person who travels farthest; the last to arrive, travels least." Sure enough, Carol was the last to arrive.

She said she was still groggy from her office Christmas party, two nights before. Miguel said everyone from his work was coming to his place next Sunday for a *tamale* fest and invited everyone in the study group to come too.

Penny wasn't working, didn't have an office party to go to, but wanted in on the conversation. She asked Harry when his office party was. He told her Saturday night. She could not avoid her mean streak or putting Harry on the spot, her gay-dar was picking up blips on Harry. She asked him who he was taking.

"I'm not sure."

"Harry, it's less than a week away. Either you have someone steady who knows your schedule better than you do, or you're going to spring an invite on someone who already has plans."

"You're right, Penny."

"I'm right. Which is it?"

"I was going to say, unless I go solo."

"Harry!"

"Give him a break, Penny," interjected Carol. "If Harry wanted to go into his private life, he would. Right, Harry?"

"Come on guys. Aren't we here to study?"

"You and I are, Harry," Miguel exclaimed forcefully, challenging the girls with a menacing look, "unless you'd rather gossip." He wagged his finger at them with a flair, leaving no doubt which team he played for.

ANOTHER ROUND OF FINALS coming up. Harry's first thought was to skip the office Christmas Party and Miguel's *tamale* fest to study. But he knew there was no way he'd do that.

Toby kept popping into his head. Their holiday schedules turned out mismatched puzzle pieces. Toby had her own flights, and was taking others, that other flight attendants wanted to give away, and she was spending a short time in Washington with her family for the holiday.

Harry and Toby set their sights on New Year's Eve.

AT SCHWARTZ & WEISS, trying not to spill his drink, Harry crossed the lobby, bouncing off people, inching his way toward his favorite attorney, Ron Cohen.

"Here he is. Hey, Harry."

"Hi, Ron."

The week before the party, Ron and Harry had been charged with putting together jury instructions for one of the partners. The problem was, neither Harry nor Ron had ever prepared jury instructions before.

Ron waxed on to a small group surrounding him at the Christmas party.

"You should have seen Harry and me last week. We were in the library looking for jury instructions for Adam's jury trial. Really sweating it. Harry's in law school and I've been a lawyer for two years. No trial experience between us. And we're working for Adam, of all taskmasters. We couldn't find jury instructions in the library. We talked about updating our resumés. After all, our incompetence was sabotaging a million-dollar case for the firm's best client.

"Well, Harry saved the day by locating what everyone calls BAJI for short. It's the Book of Approved Jury Instructions with the acronym BAJI.

"No sooner had Harry found it, when I got a call from Adam at the courthouse, just finishing the pre-trial conference. Adam told me it was going to be a bench trial, and he'd see us when he got back to the office.

"I told Harry what Adam had said, and Harry told me it was the best news he'd heard in a long time. So that's when I asked Harry if he knew what a bench trial was, *cuz* I didn't.

"'Yeah, it's a judge trial, before the judge only, no jury.'

"No jury, I repeated. Yeah, 'No jury,' he said again.

"I got giddy. I asked Harry if he'd seen the film, 'The Treasure of the Sierra Madre' with Humphrey Bogart. He nodded.

"I said, 'Remember when Fred C. Dobbs, Bogart's character, asked the Mexicans to prove they were *Federalis* by showing him their badges and they responded, 'Badges? What badges? We ain't got no badges. We don't have to show you no stinkin' badges.'

"Harry, laughing, replied 'BAJIs? What BAJIs? We ain't got no BAJIs. We don't have to do no stinkin' BAJIs for a bench trial!'

"Honest to God, we both ended up rolling on the floor of the library laughing our asses off."

When Ron finished his story, Becky joined the small group that looked like they were having a great time of it.

She wore red. She was the undisputed queen of cleavage that night, based on looks she got from not only the men, but all their wives and girlfriends. She snuck up, leaned into Harry, noticeably tipsy, and whispered, "Merry Christmas!"

"You, two," Harry said, lowering his gaze and fully protected from sexual harassment through the adept use of a homonym. Lifting his glass and his eyes, he added, "I mean Happy Hanukkah!"

No one got carded at the office Christmas party so Becky, at her tender age, was flirting not only with Harry, but with libation disaster.

Harry worked on slowing her down. But her eyes glazed over. She stuck close to him the rest of the evening. Ron kept drooling at her until his date dragged him off.

Harry was concerned about Becky driving herself home, and so was Adam, concerned about the firm's liability for supplying liquor to a minor. He asked Harry to give her a lift home, and turn in a messenger slip for it, for overtime and mileage. Harry told Adam no worries, he'd already decided to do it anyway.

HARRY AND BECKY CHATTED, Becky mostly, all the way to her house, about the party, the attorneys, the secretaries, everyone. Becky had insights into all the personalities and knew who could be counted on in a pinch and who couldn't. It was revealing. From the calls she took, she knew which attorneys were adored, which henpecked, and which ignored.

When they got near Becky's house in the Calabasas hills, it was pitch black. The headlights from Harry's car began picking up a reflective mist from thickening ground fog. Becky guided him up the hill through the last several turns and reminded him to take the same roads down. As long as he was heading down, he'd be going in the right direction.

They ended up above the fog on a bright clear night. Harry, living in LA, hadn't seen stars for a long time.

Harry stopped the car at the walkway.

Becky slurred, "No. Pull up a little, to that cluster of mailboxes."

He assumed she wanted to compose herself before facing her parents.

"Maybe we should have stopped for coffee," Harry said.

"No," she said.

She threw an arm over Harry and laid the beginning of a make-out-session kiss on him. She had sexy lips. His first reaction was *Not bad, not bad at all* but he separated once she got to the end of her first breath. He reached for his door handle, popped open the door, and said he'd walk her up. No response. He glanced over at her. He could not believe his eyes, Becky's moonlit tits.

"Whoa, Becky. This is not going to happen."

"Why not? Don't you like me?"

"Of course, I do. You're the best. But I'm going with someone."

"Oh. I didn't know that. Shoot. And now I've flashed you. I'm sorry."

"I didn't look, Becky. Honest," he lied.

Becky didn't believe Harry. Not about him having a girlfriend, she screened all his calls, and not that he hadn't snuck a look. But it was getting late and she was still woozy from drink and woozier from the long kiss. She figured throwing up on him would not advance her cause.

IT RAINED THE WEEK before Christmas. Harry's finals were over. Becky took on a more worldly air but then confided in Harry her father had arranged a date for her with a young oncologist for the Calabasas Country Club Holiday Ball and asked Harry if he thought she should wear the red dress again. Harry guffawed thinking *oncology* was *proctology*.

"What's so funny, Harry?"

"What's an oncologist?"

"A cancer doctor."

"Oh. Your red dress is great. But soak it in coffee the night before, this time."

"What?"

"So it'll stay up all night."

"Harry!"

"Remind me to give you a cartoon," he said.

"What?"

"Gotta run."

Later that day Harry grabbed a blank piece of paper out of the Xerox machine. On it, he drew a patient on an exam table with his bare butt in the air. The butt was facing a doctor who was reaching for something from his nurse who was handing him a Bud Light bottle of beer. The caption was "No! No! No! I said a butt light!"

Becky gushed, "Can I keep it? My dad'll get a big kick out of this."

Becky stayed loyal to Harry. She kept slipping him the best runs. Indeed, she acted like nothing had happened. And Harry was fine with that.

THE LA TIMES HAD an ominous front-page headline: MISSING WOMEN – HOLLYWOOD ALARMED. Up to a hundred women are reported missing every year in Hollywood. Some are victims of drugs, sex trafficking, some go back to where they came from, and some are murdered.

Harry had a research assignment in a choice-of-law case that took him to the UCLA Law Library to photocopy some Illinois statutes and the annotated cases that interpreted them.

When he was done, he asked the research librarian if the library had telephone books from around the country. No, but the downtown city library did. Next time Harry went downtown he checked out the phone book for Ogallala, Nebraska.

There were two Whiteclouds in Ogallala. Mary and Nick. Harry called them. Mary said Brigette was not in and hung up right away. Nick said it was his sister and to call Mary, his mother, who could answer any questions. He was not about to.

Harry called Detective Fields and asked him if he ever contacted Brigette's mom. The detective explained he called and told her he was on the Ogallala High School class reunion committee. He did not want to tell her anything to alarm her but just wanted to get her reaction to questions about Brigette, where she was, her latest address, phone number, see if her mom appeared to know anything, and since it appeared she didn't, he'd let it go for now.

HARRY GOT HOLD of the manager of the apartment building next door. His name was Ivan. He was bald and burly with a thick Russian accent. He smelled like a plumber by trade. He could not have been less helpful. He literally had his hand out.

"You pay me, and I tell you what I tell cop."

"Look. I got twenty bucks on me."

"You got eighty short."

"Come on, *tavaritch*," Harry said, relying on the TV commercial for Tavaritch Vodka, with tavaritch translating to comrade or friend.

The Russian met the plea with "Sto dollarov, tavaritch (a hundred bucks, pal)."

Harry caught "dollarov," combined with Ivan's sneer, and the dead eyes of a Charles Bronson character. Harry raced through his options. There was only one, with this hard-headed Rusky, pay it. Harry could threaten this guy with immigration but then spend the rest of his days waiting for a heavy wrench to the back of the head. "Look. We're neighbors. I'm just trying to do what's right. Cut me a break here."

"OK, neighbor. Where you living?"

Harry pointed to his house next door and immediatly wanted the gesture back.

"I got something you wanting. Especial. I find after cop leaving. Two hundred dollar."

"*Two* hundred? What is this?"

"Two hundred dollar you finding out."

"I won't have $200 until next month."

"See you next month, comrade."

Harry thought about calling Detective Fields. *Bad idea: one, he might not share any evidence with him; and two, Ivan would put two and two together and know who turned him over to the detective.*

TOBY CALLED HARRY and asked him if he'd mind if they didn't go out on New Year's Eve, if she just came over around eleven o'clock. She had a chance to fly New Year's Eve day and make double time, but most of the night would be gone by the time she got back.

Harry never liked New Year's Eve anyway. He typically stayed home. For him it was amateur night for drunks on the road. He pitied the pedestrians. He was all for staying in and having her come over.

"We can watch the ball drop with Dick Clark and Guy Lombardo in Times Square, in black and white, on an old portable."

"Great. It'll be nostalgic, Harry."

Harry laid out a spread for Toby. He got a pound and a half of roast beef from the deli and bolillos from the bakery. He would make guacamole and homemade tortilla chips *a la* Miguel. He got several pastries from a middle eastern market. He had beer but picked up an off-brand French champagne, forcing him to buy a corkscrew.

With all this, and toys for nieces and nephews, spring tuition, and two bills to Ivan the Terrible, he'd blown his budget. But thanks to Schwartz & Weiss his Christmas bonus saved him.

Toby called at 9 o'clock, with Harry on the brink of finishing his food prep, to say she was stuck in a snowstorm in Salt Lake City but should get out early the next morning.

There went New Year's Eve. But tomorrow was Harry's favorite football day of the year, the big Bowl Games.

"That's OK," he said.

"What are you doing tomorrow, Harry?"

"Watching football. Say, would you like to watch the Rose Bowl and Orange Bowl games tomorrow?"

"Football on TV? That's our date?"

"Uh-huh."

"Well, we'll always have "A Chorus Line.""

"Huh?"

"My place, Harry. I've got a color TV."

Harry showed up with most of the day-old spread he'd put together the night before, plus champagne and beer, around two in the afternoon. The Rose Bowl was just about to start.

Harry had a great time being Harry, sitting on the couch, watching every play, second-guessing the play-calling, and bending forward for food and drink. Toby threw a pillow on his lap and mostly slept, stretched out on the couch in jeans and a sweater under a Navajo blanket.

After hours of football, Harry woke Toby for the Orange Bowl halftime show. He asked her how her New Year's Eve had gone in Salt Lake City.

"Pretty tame I imagine," he added.

"Pretty lame. Last night we were at the hotel bar getting coke, ginger ale and seven ups for our smuggled-in mini-bottles when some drunk comes right up and says, 'I'd like to get into your pants.'"

"What'd you do, Toby?"

"I twisted my head, looked down at my backside, turned back to him and said, 'I think one asshole in there is enough.'"

Harry's laugh nearly bucked her head off the pillow.

After a moment, Harry asked Toby which airline had blue-grey uniforms.

"Pan Am."

"When I saw Cleo she was in a blue-grey uniform."

"Hmm."

AT HARRY'S STUDY GROUP everyone raved about the *tamale* fest and what a great host Miguel had been. The group was plowing ahead in the new semester. Penny took the lead on Real Property; Carol, Corporations; and, Harry, Evidence. Miguel played devil's advocate.

Harry briefed them on hearsay, in-plain-sight, fruit-of-the-poisonous-tree, and similar-crimes.

"Relevant evidence is anything that tends to prove or disprove an issue in a case," he told them. *Here was a subject*, he thought, *driven by logic and common sense.*

HARRY BUZZED the apartment manager next door. He let Harry in.

Ivan's apartment was stark. It smelled like burnt grease. There was an open toolbox on the floor to the left, a shop-vac next to it, and a knee-high plumber's-snake cannister on wheels next to that. It appeared he lived alone. Harry stood just beyond the door. The sun shone through a side window onto a table with girlie magazines on it.

Ivan held out his hand. Harry handed him two one-hundred-dollar bills. He took them, looked them over, rubbed them between his fingers and grunted. He walked to the kitchen and came back with two crumpled pieces of small paper.

He handed them to Harry. Harry looked at them. The one was yellowed and had "Brigette Whitecloud" typed on it, it was rectangular and only slightly larger than the typeset. The other was a torn piece of a receipt from Western Costume showing a total of $14.73. Harry would take them to Detective Fields.

But before he did that, he called Monica at Prudential to see if she had any new information. None, except her supervisor was in contact with LAPD and Brigette's mom. Harry asked Monica if she'd given a statement to LAPD. No, she hadn't.

Harry was on his way back from court when he swung by the station on Wilcox Avenue in Hollywood. Detective Fields was in and saw Harry right away.

"How've you been, Harry?"

"Good. Thanks. You?"

"Good. I'm glad you came in. I've got something to show you. That "Chorus Line" was quite a play. I'm glad Ella talked me into it. Toby talk you into it?"

"No. I heard it was good and wanted to take her somewhere special."

"Well, you did. What are you here for?"

"You know, I was talking to Brigette's apartment manager and he found a couple things. How or when I don't know. And I don't know if it was before or after forensics went in."

"Really? What is it?

Harry handed over an envelope with the "Brigette Whitecloud" name label and the "Western Costume" receipt in it.

Detective Fields opened the envelope and shook the contents onto his desk.

"Have you handled these?

"Yes. After the apartment manager did."

"I'm glad to hear you're on the case, Harry. Just yesterday, I called Mrs. Whitecloud and had a heart to heart with her about Brigette's disappearance. She was very upset."

"I bet. So what's next?"

Detective Fields sidestepped the question.

"This label must've been in the resident directory at the entrance to the building. What do you make of it, Harry?"

"Nothing. And I don't want to tell you what I had to go through, to get it."

"Let me get my notes." Detective Fields went to a file cabinet and pulled out a folder. He thumbed through it.

"OK. You told me there was no Cleo listed in the building. Last you saw her she told you she was going to call the police, but we both know she didn't. You went gumshoe in the building and figured out she might be Brigette. Later, Toby confirmed it."

"Right."

"OK. I'll see what Western Costume has to say about this receipt."

"I called them."

"You did?"

"I had a hunch. I told them I needed to rent a stewardess uniform. What would it cost? The answer was 'A single uniform? What airlines? How long?' I told her just one, Pan Am for one day. She said, '$7.95.'"

"Nice try, Harry. Close, but no cigar. The math is off. $7.95 – 1 day, $15.90 – 2 days, $23.85 – 3 days. I'll look into it, Harry."

"You're quite the math whiz but I wasn't finished, Detective."

"Call me Teddy."

"Thanks. So then I said . . ."

Teddy cut him off, "So then you said, "How much for a two-day rental?"

"Right. And she said, 'For 2 days the rate goes down to $6.95, 5 days $4.95.'"

"What does that tell you, Harry?"

"Two days at $6.95 is $13.90. There's a six percent sales tax. Total, $14.73. Same amount as the receipt. The receipt was in Brigette's apartment. Cleo wore the uniform. Cleo is Brigette. So, I confirmed what we already knew, and I did not find out anything new."

"Bingo. That's often the case. New leads lead to old news. I'll see if she used a credit card.

"Say. What about her banking activity?"

"Off the record to you, Harry, no activity since the day she went missing."

"What about Prudential. Did she have a life insurance policy?"

"You sure you want to become a lawyer? I can put in a good word for you and get you into the police academy. Next class starts February 1st. Not only that, Harry, the academy cafeteria serves the best clam chowder in the city every Friday for lunch."

"Don't think I haven't considered it."

"No. No insurance policy."

"Based on the receipt and the name label, what do you think, Harry?"

"I think, all it proves is Brigette rented a stewardess uniform. But here's the kicker, or the *kinker*, she wore it for Offramp's lead singer."

"Take a look at this DMV photo, Harry."

"That's Cleo."

"That's Brigette. And she's still out there, Harry, if she's alive."

Switching gears, Detective Fields asked Harry if he had Super Bowl plans.

"No."

"You a football fan?"

"Big time."

"What about Toby? She a football fan?"

"Not hardly."

"Oh. Do you think she might like to keep Ella company while you and I watch the game on the big screen. I just got a 25" RCA color television set."

"Sounds great. I'll let you know."

"RON COHEN HAS BEEN LOOKING all over for you," Becky said, when Harry returned to the office.

"Thanks."

"And Harry you need to file something in federal court before 4:30. It's for Jacob. Barbara should have it ready soon. She asked specifically for you, so you might want to let her know you're back."

"Sure. Thanks, Becky."

Harry swung by Barbara's station. She was going 90 words a minute on her IBM Selectric. Harry told her he'd be in Ron's office, or the library, when she was ready for the run to federal court.

Ron's door was open. He was on the phone but motioned Harry to come in and take a seat.

"OK. OK. OK. OK," Ron said, before hanging up. He had a big smile on his face. He slid open the middle drawer to his desk and put his hand inside it.

"Guess what I've got?"

"A complete set of BAJI?"

"No."

"A 'Treasure of the Sierra Madre' movie poster?"

"No."

"The new Linda Ronstadt album?"

"No."

"OK, I give."

"Harry, before I show you, I've got to ask you a question about Becky."

Harry started shaking his head no.

"Come on Harry."

Holding up empty hands and shaking them like they were holding maracas, he went on, "Tă, dă dă -- tă, dă, dă -- the Lady in Red. Did you get a load of that rack?"

If you only knew, Harry mused to himself, but kept shaking his head no.

"Harry! I just want to know if she's going with someone. You seem to know her pretty well."

Harry kept shaking his head.

"I'm thinking about asking her to the Super Bowl."

"Super Bowl?"

"Damn straight!" Ron dropped his phantom maracas, reached into his desk drawer, and started waving Super Bowl tickets shamelessly in Harry's face.

"And you'd rather take Becky than me?"

"Not so fast, Chuck Yeager! Can't you count?"

There were four tickets when he separated them.

"Me. Becky, you and whoever you want to take."

"Geez, Ron. I can't believe it. What do I owe you?"

"Not on your life. They're yours. Who you gonna take? And don't tell me you wanna take Becky."

"No. I think you two would make a great match. I'm not sure who I'll take. I have to think about it. But Ron. These tickets are gold. Gold, Ron. You should take the partners. It's the best career move you could make."

"You're right, Harry, I should," he said, nodding his head and looking convinced.

"Here."

Ron handed two tickets to Harry, smiled, and shooed him out of the office.

⁘

RON AND BECKY were sitting midway up the stands at the Rose Bowl on the 30-yard line, with two empty seats next to them, only minutes to kick-off. They saw a black man making his way down the row toward them, and he took the seat two down from Becky.

Ron leaned way back and whispered something into Becky's ear.

"Scalped?" she blurted out.

Still past upright, Ron said, "Shush, I'll tell you later."

During the National Anthem, Harry waited in the aisle at attention. When it finished, he shimmied his way down the row.

"Hi Ron, hi Becky, have you met Teddy?"

"No."

"I didn't want to bother them until you got here," Teddy said.

"Teddy, this is Ron and Becky."

It turned out no one liked the Raiders, but all four of them put that aside for the day and cheered them on. Ron was a 49er fan; Becky, Rams; Harry, Chargers; and, Teddy, Redskins. But between California and Minnesota, they went with the California team.

Big winners that day -- the Raiders, Ron, Becky, Harry, and Teddy; arguably, bigger winners, Ella and Toby.

During the game Ron asked Teddy what percentage of crimes he was able to solve. Teddy said it was hard to tell because the big stuff often took a long time and a lot of effort, while the petty stuff either got solved right away or went by the wayside.

"It must be emotionally draining," Becky said.

The comment triggered Teddy to bring up a hit and run case with two fatalities. In early August there had been a hit and run on Melrose Avenue, a mother and her three-year old child were run down in a crosswalk.

Harry remembered reading about it in the newspaper. Becky said she heard it on TV, and couldn't get over the commentary, the mother and child were sent airborne and the mother never let go of the child's hand.

DETECTIVE FIELDS took another stab at the Melrose hit and run. He had patrol officers spend an hour, before and after the time of the incident on the same day of the week, talk to passersby both on foot and in cars.

He planned to run the operation over three straight weeks. He hit paydirt the first day. The chef for Chianti was stopped on the sidewalk by police and asked if he knew anything about the hit and run in August.

He said he was on his way to work walking on Melrose Avenue when up ahead he saw the mother and child step into the crosswalk at Fuller, after the light went red on Melrose, green on Fuller. They took a few steps and a car plowed into them sending them into the air. The car whizzed by and he saw the license plate. He raced to the stricken mother and child. He kept repeating the license plate number to himself. The car was metallic grey in color. He later picked out a BMW 2500 at the station.

He said he focused on the license plate. The driver was a blonde. The sun reflected off the windshield hiding the driver's face. The chef zeroed in on the license plate.

He talked to an officer right after the accident. The chef told the officer he was late for work. The officer told him he could go to the restaurant and the officer would see him later for his statement. The officer never showed up. The chef figured they got what they needed from others.

He wrote down the license plate number when he got to work. Now the writing is gone. He remembered an "M" an "X" and an "L" but only one number for sure, "5."

HARRY AND TOBY went on a cheap date to the Gordon Theater on La Brea for a double feature to see "Silver Streak" and

"Carwash" both starring Richard Pryor. They liked "Carwash" better. It was nonstop laughs, a parade of oddball characters, and deftly plotted. Harry said it was the funniest picture he'd seen since "Smile," but Toby hadn't seen that one. After the movie they went to Harry's place to let Boomer out, then back to Toby's.

They made love twice. Toby told him that never happened before.

It was their first night and Harry did not want it to end.

"Go ahead, rub it. The third time's the charm. You can hop on and go for three."

And she did.

Next night Harry used his tongue to curl her toes.

The night after that, they took Boomer for a run on the beach in Santa Monica. Once back in the parked Mazda, with traffic whizzing by them on Pacific Coast Highway and Harry stiff-arming Boomer to keep him at bay, Toby brought Harry with her mouth. Suddenly, doggy-style took on an added meaning for Harry.

Next day Harry called Toby and asked her when her lease was up. She said it was month-to-month. He asked her if she wanted to move in. She told him to wait -- thinking nothing *that* good could last.

Toby told Harry she grew up poor. Her dad was a fisherman. They always had enough to eat. But her dad and uncles drank.

Her mother died when she was nine and she had to help raise three younger children. Her brother followed in the footsteps of his dad and uncles. Her two sisters were different as night and day. The older of the two was into drugs early in high school, and now saddled with three children, no husband.

But hand it to her, she got clean last year and got into community college. Toby could not have been more proud of her than when she saw her over Christmas. Toby helps her with money.

Her younger sister is a junior at the University of Washington, an English major. Toby helps her with money, too.

Toby, herself, wanted to leave home as soon as she could. After high school she applied to Alaska Airlines and Western Airlines. Both wanted to hire her. She went with Western, to fly to more cities and get based in Los Angeles. Besides Western was the o-o-only way to fly!

Toby was constantly hit on, went out occasionally, but never met anyone like Harry. It looked and felt like the two of them were in love.

She worked as much as she could and lived frugally. She was a clean freak. She loved the rain and that's what she missed most in LA. She read everything on the NY Times' Best Seller List and feminist authors. She had no interest in sports or the law but did not begrudge Harry his. In fact, she liked how they complemented each other. She liked Motown and Jazz. She also liked the glamour of flying, meeting new and interesting people, and palling around with other stewardesses.

In contrast to her life in the fast lane, she was never lonely, only alone, when she curled up by herself at home. She loved her solitude.

She surprised herself with Harry. The sex was something else. She did things with him she never imagined. She felt awakened by it. Harry was the guy for her.

Harry loved everything about Toby. She was above all, kind and good, unlike Harry's first love. Harry marveled at Toby's every movement, her sense of humor, her banter, her intellect, and every inch of her. Her skin was the rich color of cinnamon and satin to the touch. He was never so turned on by anyone.

BECKY CALLED HARRY in the library. "Got a second?"

"Sure. What's up?"

Becky whispered, "Can you meet me at The Pub after work?"

"Sure."

The Pub was under the building they worked in, next to a news stand at the entrance to a massive multi-level underground parking garage. Harry found Becky in a far corner of the bar nursing a Pellegrino. She looked concerned.

"Hi, Becky."

"Hey, Harry."

"Why the intrigue?"

"It's Ron."

Harry started shaking his head no.

"I can't get rid of him."

Harry lowered his head.

"Harry? Harry!"

"Yes, Becky?"

"What should I do?"

"Becky, I don't want to get into the middle of this. You know how fond I am of both of you."

"That's why I asked you, Harry."

"Come on, Becky. It's between you and Ron. You need to talk to Ron."

"I have. He won't listen."

"He really likes you."

"Harry. I hate to ask, but would you tell him?"

"Tell him what?"

"Tell him I can't go out with him"

"Geez, Becky. Why don't *you* tell him?"

The waitress arrived and looked at Harry.

"I'll have a butt light." He emphasized the word "butt."

Becky started laughing. Despite his effort, the waitress heard Bud Light.

"That's it?"

"No. Make it a Guinness."

Turning to Becky, she asked, "You OK with your water?"

"Yes."

Harry tapped Becky on the arm. "Becky! That's the ticket. Tell Ron you met a young, handsome proctologist."

"And I've fallen head over heels for him."

"No. Ass over tea kettle. Ron'll appreciate the irony."

"Harry!"

"Look. I'm sorry you don't want to date Ron. He's smitten."

"Really? What has he told you?"

"He hasn't told me a thing. We don't talk like women talk."

"I find that hard to believe. Not one mention of me?"

"No," Harry lied.

"You're covering for him. I know it."

"No, Becky."

"You sure he never told you I had a great rack and asked you if you thought I'd go out with him?"

Harry turned beet red.

"That guy can't keep his mouth shut. If he had broken the Japanese Code during World War II, instead of using it against Japan, he would've bragged about it to Tokyo Rose."

"Harry, *you*'ve never talked about me to anyone."

"No. And you can take that to the bank."

⊰⊱

THE DYNAMICS AT work changed for a couple weeks. Becky still gave Harry the good runs but was noticeably aloof. Ron pouted. Harry knew he'd get blamed by the both of them. But it only lasted a short while and soon everything went back on an even keel.

Harry got a call from Detective Fields.

"Valentine's Day, Harry. It's coming up. I'm sure you and Toby want to be alone, but I've got tickets to "Bubbling Brown Sugar" at the Pantages. Would you two like to go?"

"You bet. Let me check with Toby."

"Great."

"Anything new on Brigette Whitecloud?"

"Her mom sent me photos. And she asked me about her life insurance policy. I told her I was unaware of one. Her mom said she had a $500,000 policy with Mutual of Omaha. And her mom wanted a declaration of missing and presumed dead. I told her the case was still open and I could not do that for her. Not yet. And I hoped we'd find her."

"Is it possible Brigette is in on an insurance scam? She was in the business, working for Prudential but insured by Mutual of Omaha. Do you think her mother is in on it?"

"I don't know, Harry."

———— ❖ ————

BEFORE THE PLAY Teddy led everyone into an old Hollywood watering hole called "The Stage Door Canteen" two doors down from the Pantages Theater entrance on Hollywood Boulevard.

The old-time bar had a high art deco ceiling. Three glass-and-steel lamps with low-watt industrial bulbs in them hung from the ceiling filling the place with a dull bronze aura.

There were a lot of black theatergoers in the bar, foreshadowing the show's setting, a Harlem nightclub over a span of two decades.

The music and energy in the play electrified the audience. The female vocalist-dancer stole the show.

Teddy, Ella and Toby were light years ahead of Harry when it came to Duke Ellington, Eubie Blake, Cab Calloway, Count Basie and Fats Waller.

After the musical, they all went to Fatburger at La Cienega and San Vicente on the edge of Beverly Hills, for burgers, fries and sweet potato pie. The owner of Fatburger greeted Teddy and Ella like old friends and made Harry and Toby feel like new ones.

Teddy brought everyone up to speed on the hit and run case and was now trying to match a partial license plate.

Teddy switched gears to the missing-person case. Toby was interested to hear about Brigette and recounted for Teddy how she'd met Brigette and the times she saw her. That segued into the *How I Met Harry* story.

Ella wanted to know what Offramp was like. Toby said the bass player was a quiet guy, the drummer was a crackup, the keyboard guy was intense, and the lead guitar-lead singer was incredibly arrogant, and his pipes weren't all that great. The bass and keyboard wrote the music and lyrics.

The lead seemed annoyed at Brigette that night. She said she was going out with him. But Toby didn't know how long that lasted. The night Toby saw Offramp she was with a crew of five stewardesses all Clairoled-up and pushed-up who seemed to have captured the fancies of all the musicians. That left Brigette and Toby third wheels when the session ended near dawn.

Teddy asked Toby for any details she recalled.

"Brigette was there when we got there. She was angry when we left, and she drove *his* car. She knew the valet. He grabbed the keys for her and came back with the car."

"Did she ever mention the lead singer over the next year?"

"No. And I never asked."

"Do you know anyone else she dated?"

"No."

Talk turned to the show. Toby asked Ella what her favorite number was.

"I liked so many of them but probably *Sweet Georgia Brown*. No, *Honeysuckle Rose*. I'll be singing them around the house all next week."

"You sing and dance?"

"Church choir. I dance, but not like Georgia Brown does."

Harry shook his head, and said, "Too bad, Teddy."

Three pairs of eyes rolled at him at the same time.

With Harry now outcast, Toby asked Ella if she did anything musical with her 5th graders?

"The whole school does a little Christmas show, and one in the Spring."

"What kind of songs in the Spring?"

"Upbeat Motown and a few Broadway show tunes."

"I'd love to see it."

"You're invited. You too, Harry."

DETECTIVE FIELDS decided to take all the interviews of the car owners with potential matching plates. Because they were BMWs they were in the better parts of town.

Everyone was cooperative. They'd tell him where they worked, their usual driving routes, and lastly if and when they'd been in Hollywood. They allowed Detective Fields to take a look at their cars. Any damage was documented and it either predated or postdated the hit and run.

Damage to the car always bothered Detective Fields. The woman was slight and the child was just three. If impact was mainly on soft tissue the BMW could keep the secret.

Detective Fields made it through the list of license plates without the hit he'd hoped for.

TOBY FINISHED HER LAST LEG in Salt Lake City. It was early enough to grab a cab with the girls and go downtown for dinner. Gloria Sanchez, a Utah native, guided the group to the Guadalupe Center and the La Morena Café. The food was mouthwatering.

From there she took everyone to D.B. Cooper's, a private club, where members could bring in hard liquor and wine for a corkage fee. The State only allowed hard liquor sales at State liquor stores, not in restaurants or bars. Private clubs were the exception.

Western stewardesses used to joke that the in-flight welcome-to-Salt-Lake-City announcement should have been "Don't forget, turn your watches ahead an hour and your minds back a hundred years."

Gloria's brother was a waiter at D.B. Cooper's and got her and her stewardess friends into the club that night.

Toby asked Sharon Moran if she remembered the night at Capitol Records.

"I sure do."

"Do you remember the beautiful dark-haired girl that was there?"

"Vaguely. I don't remember talking to her. Wasn't she going with one of the guys in the band?"

"The lead singer. You know I left in the morning when everyone was talking about going out to breakfast," Toby said.

"Yeah. We went to Oscar's on Sunset. I went home after that, but Viv and Carly took off to the lead singer's place in Laurel Canyon to flop by the pool all day."

"I haven't been paired with Viv in a long time."

"She quit."

"Really?"

"Rumor has it she got pregnant, wanted to keep it, and moved in with her mom?"

"Where?"

"Somewhere in the Valley."

"Did anyone ever tell you anything about the lead singer?"

"You mean like how good he was, or what a douchebag he could be?"

"Yeah."

"After the session at Capitol Records, Viv told me the lead singer asked her out. She went out with him. She was non-plussed."

"Is he the father?"

"Oh, no. It's Perry Hartney."

"Captain Hartney?

"Mm-hmm."

"Does his wife know?"

"I don't think so."

"These pilots."

TOBY TOLD HARRY what she'd uncovered in Salt Lake City.

"Do you think you can find out where Viv lives?" Harry asked her.

"I think so."

Toby did, and Harry forwarded the information to Teddy.

VIV'S MOM SAW Detective Fields through the screen door, coming up the driveway. She quickly latched the screen door and spoke to him through it.

"Good afternoon, Ma'am. I'm Detective Fields from the Los Angeles Police Department."

"Yes."

"I'm here to see Vivian Nielsen."

"She's out."

"Oh. When will she be back?"

"I don't know."

"Is she at work?"

"No."

"Here's my card. He placed it between the frame and the screen. Would you ask her to call me?"

"What's this about?"

"Nothing for her to worry about. It's a routine investigation."

Walking away Detective Fields heard, "Hey" behind him. "What do you need?"

Viv had pushed the screen door wide open. She stood a foot taller than her mother. If she was pregnant, she wasn't showing.

"Just a few questions. Shouldn't take long. We can talk out here or inside."

"Sure," she said, distancing herself from her mother, and closing the gap toward Detective Fields.

"Do you recall seeing Offramp at Capitol Records?"

"Yes. My crew got invited by their manager. Offramp was making an album."

"Did you go out for breakfast afterwards?"

"Yes."

'Remember where?"

"Sunset near Highland. Ozzie's?"

"Did you go to the lead singer's house after that?"

She turned back to see her mom in the doorway behind the screen. "Let's move down a little," she said.

"We hung out most of the day at the pool."

"Did you swim?"

"Yes."

'Did you bring your swimsuit?"

"No. He had a bunch of bikinis in the cabana."

"How many girls were there?"

"Two of us."

"What was the other girl's name?"

"Carly. Carly Magnusen."

"Do you remember what color bikinis the two of you wore?"

"I think she wore a coral floral." She paused and smiled at the rhyme she made. "I still have mine. It's a dark teal. They both were brand new, still had the tags on them."

"Do you know if Carly ever went out with any bandmember?"

"She went out with Arnie. He's the lead singer."

"By the way, do you remember the names of the other girls at the all-night session?"

"Terry Knight, Sharon Moran and Toby Maize."

"Did they go to the pool?"

"No."

"Did you ever go out with a bandmember?"

"Arnie."

"How many times? And where?"

"Once. Are you after him?"

"No. I'm looking for a missing person. Do you remember a girl at the all-night session, not a stewardess, who was there when you arrived?"

"Yes. I met her."

"Do you remember her name?"

"No."

"Have you seen her since?"

"No."

"Do you know what her relationship to the band was?"

"Arnie told me she was a groupie."

"When did he tell you that?"

"When I went out with him, I asked him about her."

"Why'd you do that?"

"He told me he never went out with anyone. He was only about music. And I was very special to him."

"Did you believe him?"

"Not at all."

"How would you describe him?"

"What he looks like?"

"No. His personality."

"He doesn't have one. No sense of humor. Self-absorbed. A bit kinky."

Detective Fields had penetrating dark eyes. Flashing them sometimes was more effective than a follow-up question.

"Look. We had sex. One time. He wanted me to meet him at the Radisson next to the airport. 'Come straight over after your flight,' he said, 'for room service and drinks. Then we'll go out.' I went."

"And?"

"We never got out. He wanted me to take off my underwear and leave on my uniform. I had a flight early the next morning and spent half the night back at my hotel handwashing my uniform with Ivory Soap and blow-drying it with my hairdryer. It was dry clean only. I told everyone I'd hung it on the curtain rod in the shower, I'd drawn a bath, and it fell in.

"He was a big mistake. Creepy, really."

CARLY MAGNUSEN looked like a model. Tall. Thin. Perfect smile, perfect teeth. Frizzy strawberry blonde hair, bright blue eyes, and flawless skin. She had everything.

Almost everything.

When she moved into her first apartment with two other stewardesses, they scoured the place with Spic and Span. Carly was scrubbing under the kitchen sink, but with little success. Her roommate told her she had to use elbow grease. Carly spent the next ten minutes going through all the cleaning supplies but couldn't find it.

Arnie told her she could be a model and make lots of money. He brought a professional photographer to his house, plied Carly with liquor, and had her shot in all sorts of costumes. She passed out that night but woke up in an LAPD woman officer's uniform.

"The navy blue one?" Detective Fields asked.

"Yes."

"Did you have the holster?"

"No."

"Nylons?"

"No."

"Underwear?"

"No. And my top was wide open, and my skirt was up to my waist."

"Did you report this to the police?"

"No."

"Would you like to report it now."

"No."

"Why not?"

"I'm afraid of what he might do."

"Did he threaten you?"

She paused for a long time.

"No. Not really. No. He never said anything to me."

"Do you remember the recording session at Capitol Records?"

"Yes."

"Who was there? Which stewardesses?"

"Viv, Toby, Sharon and Terry."

"Did you see another girl there with dark hair?"

"Yes."

"Did you talk to her?"

"No. But she offered me a drink."

"Did you take it?"

"Yes."

"How old are you?"

"20."

"How old were you then?"

"19."

"What kind of drink was it?"

"Coffee."

TEDDY WANTED TO BOUNCE things off Harry. Harry asked him if he took notes of the witness interviews. Always. He was getting the latest ones typed up.

Harry asked Teddy if he could get a copy of them and review them with his study group. Teddy thought that was a good idea and told Harry he could pick the notes up the next day.

Harry reviewed Teddy's notes. He spotted Arnie's inconsistencies. He took the notes to work and made three copies of them. On Sunday, he asked his study group if they wanted to go over a police detective's notes and see what conclusions they could draw.

Miguel was first to point out the loose ends. The Jensen lies. Carol wondered if the bass player, Bryan, knew more than he'd said, and if he was trying to sabotage Arnie. Peggy got hung up on Arnie's sexually driven costume fetish.

They thought the *four Vicodin* and *Brigette upset* was key.

Harry called Teddy and they went over everything in detail.

DETECTIVE FIELDS went to the home of Bryan Grady, the bass player for Offramp. It was on Cherokee Avenue in Hancock Park near the Wilshire Country Club. It was old, French Provincial, built in the 1930s. Detective Fields sat in the vaulted living room and marveled at the music awards and art deco prints, statues and furnishings there.

"You know it's hard for me to link these surroundings to a rock star."

"I did my time in garage bands but went on to study music in a conservatory. It's fair to say I put up with Rock and Roll and Rock and Rollers to pay the bills. If we hadn't had the immediate success we did, I'd be very happy to be a studio musician.

"And for these things here," he said, pointing around the room, "they are vintage. I picked them up over the last couple years from a shop on Melrose called 'Thanks for the Memories.'"

"Very nice." Pausing for a second, "I heard you write the music and arrange for the group."

"With Joey. Don't get me wrong, I'm proud of Offramp."

"You should be. I've always liked your music."

"Thanks, Detective. Now what can I do for you."

"You know I'm trying to find Brigette Whitecloud."

"Yes."

"I couldn't get much out of Mr. Jensen. He said she was a groupie and he only saw her at concerts and motels, and forgot she was at a recording session."

"That's Arnie."

"You seemed to know more about her than he did."

Silence. Detective Fields was inviting a voluntary response. All he got was a shrug.

"You see, Mr. Grady. She's missing. I can't rule out foul play."

"Mm-hmm."

"Do you know what made her so upset when Mr. Jensen asked you to give her four Vicodin."

"No. I couldn't get it out of her."

"Did you think she was in danger?"

"No."

"Have *you* ever taken four Vicodin?"

"No."

"How'd she react to the Vicodin."

"She calmed down and went to sleep."

"At Mr. Jensen's?"

"Yes."

"Did she wake up?"

"Not while I was there."

"And this was in early August?"

"Late July, early August."

"Before or after Elvis died?"

"Before."

"And that was the last time you saw her?"

"Last time."

"When you went to Mr. Jensen's that day, did you arrive before or after Mr. Jensen?"

"Before."

"And did Brigette and Mr. Jensen arrive together?"

"Yes."

"Where were they coming from?"

"I don't know."

"Now are you sure that that was the last time you saw her?"

"Yes."

"Did you ever ask, or did Mr. Jensen ever say, what happened to her?"

"I asked him."

"What did he say?"

"He told me she dropped out of sight."

"And when was that?"

"Last fall. Exactly when, I don't know."

"Do you know anyone else who might shed some light on this?"

"Besides Arnie?"

"Besides him."

"No."

"If you hear anything, would you give me a call?"

"I'd be glad to. I really hope you find her. She was a good person."

That last remark did not sit well with Detective Fields. *Did he say* was, *thinking back on when he knew her, or because he knows, she no longer* is.

DETECTIVE FIELDS barely convinced a judge to issue a warrant for Arnold Jensen's phone, bank and credit card records going back a year. His lawyer didn't object. The records did not reflect any tie to Brigette and only corroborated Jensen's admission regarding Sunset Boulevard motels.

Detective Fields called Harry to keep him in the loop.

"Harry, no luck with the warrants."

"Could she be in contact with her mom?"

"Her mom says no."

"Can you get her mom's phone records?"

"I asked the district attorney about that. Based on the facts so far and our ability to block any determination of death, and shield the insurance company, he did not think it was worth it.

No one sees this case as important as you or me. And I don't think I can justify going forward with this unless I catch a break."

"Makes sense."

"Let's keep in touch."

"For sure."

HARRY HAD AN IDEA but it put him in an ethical dilemma. He wanted Toby to call Mrs. Whitecloud pretending to be Brigette. He did not want Mrs. Whitecloud to go into shock, or have a stroke over the news, but he thought the call would answer the questions if Brigette was alive, if her mom was in contact with her, or if they were plotting against Mutual of Omaha, or not.

Toby didn't think it was a good idea. She didn't think she sounded enough like Brigette to pull it off. She didn't want to land in Sybil Brand with all the other female felons.

Harry thought of calling from a phone booth next to heavy traffic to muffle Toby's voice. Toby wanted a script, depending on what Mrs. Whitecloud's answers were. Toby and Harry talked about what was the best time to call, best day of the week. Harry decided to record it.

"Hello."

"Mom?"

"Who is this?"

"It's Brigette."

"Tell me your birth date."

Toby hung up.

"Busted," Harry said.

Mrs. Whitecloud chalked it up to an insurance-fraud investigation tactic.

DETECTIVE FIELDS, unaware of Harry's antics, made a legitimate call to Mrs. Whitecloud.

"Hello."

"Mrs. Whitecloud?"

"Yes."

"This is Detective Fields, Los Angeles Police Department."

"Yes."

"We haven't found Brigette, but I have a few questions I'd like you to help me with."

"OK."

"Before she went missing, was she dating anyone you were aware of?"

"No. It was pulling teeth to find out anything from Brigette. She left Nebraska for Hollywood and she did not want her mother to know anything about her."

"How did you know about her life insurance policy?"

"I got it for her when she turned 21. The premium was at the employee rate. I work for Mutual of Omaha, I'm the secretary to the local agent, and have been, for over twenty years."

"And, you came to the conclusion that she had been killed before you submitted your claim under penalty of perjury?"

"I had a terrible feeling about all of this."

"Did she ever mention, or have you ever heard, the name Arnold Jensen?"

"Say it again."

"Arnold Jensen?"

"No."

"Did she ever talk about the rock band, Offramp?"

"No."

"OK, Mrs. Whitecloud. Thank you. One more thing."

"Yes."

"Would you be willing to send me copies of your phone bills over the past six months?"

"Yes. I can do that."

"Could you also send me your phone bills from work?"

"I'd have to ask. But I think I can."

"All right, Mrs. Whitecloud. I want you to know we are doing our best to find your daughter."

"Thank you, Detective."

HARRY SAT IN the conference room at work with a number of employees. It was Friday Happy Hour at the firm, the last Friday of the month. The credenza, half the length of the conference room table, held liquor bottles, wine bottles, small buckets of ice, larger buckets of ice filled with bottles and cans of beer, cheeses and crackers.

Adam, looking to start early with a glass of Scotch, had cornered Becky alone in the darkened conference room twenty minutes before when she was setting up for the happy-hour party. He bemoaned the fact that he'd just gotten off the phone with a flaky client who wasn't paying his bills.

Becky asked who it was. Adam said it was nothing for her to worry her pretty little head about. He told Becky the client told him he'd send a check right away. But then Adam asked Becky if she knew what the two biggest lies in the world were? What? *The check's in the mail* and *I won't come in your mouth.* Becky knew best when not to react to certain things she heard from men. One thing she was beginning to learn, none of them had any limits.

Within the hour, Becky put the switch board on mobile and ended up near the conference room phone next to Harry and Ron for Happy Hour. Ron took Becky's presence at first, as a renewed chance for him, but he quickly concluded, for Becky, it had been Harry all along, when in fact, her proximity to both Ron and Harry was dictated by the location of the conference room phone, in case any calls came in. She was still on the clock.

After an hour, folks were heading out. The stragglers included the younger attorneys, the single secretaries, Ron, Harry, Becky and Adam. Harry and Ron decided to go to The Pub. Becky said she was heading home. When the three of them got up to leave, they waved to the group and thanked Adam.

"You safe to drive home, Becky? I'm on my way to Tarzana if you need a lift?"

"No thanks, Adam."

"Night you guys."

TOBY SAID SHE'D do it, but it was the last time. No more phony phone calls.

"About four in the afternoon," Harry suggested.

"It'll give Arnie time to get up and brush his teeth. But seriously, we don't want him to go after her. On second thought, Harry, I don't think we should do this at all."

"How else do we get Arnie to make a move?"

"This isn't right, Harry."

"You're still gun shy from the call to Mrs. Whitecloud."

"And you're still willing to break the law to see if the law was broken."

"OK. I give. You're right. You couldn't be righter."

TEDDY STUDIED his notes. It was clear to him Arnie lied about having Brigette in his house, his Vicodin request of Bryan, and his failure to fess up about costumes. Teddy also believed Arnie knew where she lived, even though he denied it.

"Harry, I'd like you to come along when I interview Arnold Jensen again."

"Sure."

"Look. It's unconventional. I'll introduce you as my deputy."

"OK. What should I wear?"

"Do you have a light-colored suit?"

"I've got a grey one."

"Good. I'll pick you up Wednesday at 3."

"OK."

"You might want to review the Jensen file I gave you."

"MY LAWYER SAYS this is the last time you are going to question me."

"That's right, Mr. Jensen. Thanks for letting us come by. This is Harry McHugh, my deputy."

Arnie nodded.

"Mr. Jensen, other witnesses say Ms. Whitecloud was seen in your house."

"Mm-hmm."

"I thought you told me she never came here."

"I'm not sure. Maybe she did."

"You said you didn't know where she lived."

"I didn't."

"What kind of car do you drive?"

"Porsche 911."

"Color?"

"Forest green."

"Year?"

"'77."

"Did you ever tell Bryan to give Brigette four Vicodin?"

"Look. She might have asked me for Vicodin. I might have said something to Bryan like do you have a Vicodin *for* Brigette. But I don't remember."

"Did she ever get upset to the point where she was crying?"

"Not that I remember."

"How would you describe her personality?"

"She was mostly nice."

"What about when she took your car?"

"She was on the warpath a little that day. But she brought it back when I asked."

"Did she bring it back that same day?"

"I think I waited a day or two."

"Do you remember why she didn't bring it back the same day?"

"No."

"Did you have any stewardesses over for a swim during the time frame when she had your car?"

"I don't know."

"Do you know a Viv or Vivian Neilsen?"

"I don't know."

"Did you ever meet a stewardess at the Radisson Hotel near the airport?"

"I don't know anything about that."

"Do you know a Carly Magnusen?"

"No."

"Did you ever have a photo-shoot at your home for a young woman?"

"No."

"Did Brigette return the car to you?"

"I don't remember."

"Do you remember going to her place to pick up the car?"

"No."

"Well did you have someone drive you somewhere so you could get the car from her?"

"I don't know."

"Didn't she drive the car here and you drove her home after that?"

"I think I drove her to a motel on Sunset."

"After that, did she walk home? How did she get home?"

"I might have dropped her near Willoughby."

"Willoughby and what?"

"I don't know those streets very well."

"Willoughby and McCadden, maybe?"

"I don't know."

Harry interrupted, asking Jensen if he could use the phone.

"Go ahead. It's over there."

"We'll wait 'til he gets back," Detective Fields told Jensen.

The house had canyon views, floor to ceiling windows. There was a pool cut into the slope below the house and a tennis court clinging to the hillside.

Harry finished dialing.

"Hello."

"Toby?"

"Are you done?"

"No. I'm here at Jensen's."

"What's up?'

"What kind of car did Jensen have? The one Brigette drove you in?"

"A 450 SL."

"What year?"

"Don't know."

"Thanks. I'll talk to you later."

Harry made his way back to where he was sitting.

Detective Fields continued.

"Did Brigette tell you where she was from?"

"No. Or, I mean, if she did, I don't remember."

"How many women were you seeing when you were seeing her?"

Jensen smiled. "Come on, Detective, not that."

"Ballpark?"

"Seven or eight, depending on turnover."

"Did they all wear uniforms?"

"Mostly didn't wear much."

"Ever bonk a stewardess?"

"Probably."

"Did Brigette ever dress like a stewardess?"

"I don't think so."

"What about a pirate?"

"No. I don't remember that."

"OK. Thanks for your time." Turning to Harry, "Do you have anything?"

"Mr. Jensen, do you have any cars besides the Porsche?"

"No."

"Did you have a different car when you met with Brigette at the motels?"

"I had a Mercedes."

"What year and model?"

"450 SL '76."

"What'd you do with it?"

"Trade-in."

"What dealer?"

"Porsche of Beverly Hills."

"Thank you."

DRIVING BACK TO Harry's, Detective Fields said Jensen lied about everything, but they were stymied.

"But" Harry countered, "it looks like Arnie made it all the way to Brigette's apartment. Remember I told you she got out of a Mercedes sport coupe when I saw her that morning, the day after Elvis died? That's a 450 SL."

"Assume she spent the night with him in her stewardess uniform. He drops her off early the next morning. What happened that night to compel her to go missing?"

"Don't know. The four Vicodin event took place in early August or even late July according to Bryan Grady."

"What are you going to do?"

"I don't know. We are running out of options."

"Do you think Arnie was dumping her and that brought out the crying scene?"

"Based on the timeline, they're still together for another two weeks after that."

"No. Something happened that she could not tell anyone, not even Bryan. At first, Bryan answered that he thought she feared Arnie if she told. At Bryan's second interview, he said he did not think she was afraid of Arnie."

DETECTIVE FIELDS PUT a phone call into Bryan Grady.

"Mr. Grady, that day when Brigette was upset, why were you at Mr. Jensen's before him?"

"He'd called me and asked me if I'd drop something off."

"Recreational drugs?"

After a silent pause, "Yes."

"Who's your supplier?"

"Do I have to say?"

"Yes."

"A guy named Ricardo."

"His telephone number?"

"(213) 655-6690."

"Now, you told me at the Troubadour you thought Brigette was afraid of Arnie because of what happened. But at your house you told me you didn't think she was afraid of him. Which is it?"

"I'm not sure. She seemed to be in shock."

"Shock?"

"Yeah."

"Did you ever see her, or any other Jensen girl look like they were in shock?"

"No."

"OK. If you remember anything, call me."

"I will, Detective."

SPRING BREAK, Easter and Passover converged. Harry and Toby headed for Seattle. Toby worked the flights up and back and got a friend of hers in management to comp Harry's round-trip ticket. They rented a car in Seattle and drove down to Elma.

The northwest was big, green and clean. The sense of smell, lost in LA, came alive in Washington. Ocean Shores and Quinault made up the day trips for Harry, Toby, her sisters Mary and Hildy, and Mary's kids. Toby's family treated Harry like family. The day before returning, the men took Harry out pre-dawn to dusk on their fishing boat.

Toby's family asked Harry about his own. Harry told them his dad and mom retired to Alexandria, Virginia. His dad had put in twenty- five years in the Navy. He'd been a World War II veteran, a Navy pilot with twenty-seven combat missions.

He'd taught at Pensacola and flown every fixed and rotary-wing aircraft the Navy had. Now he taught high school math.

His mother was also a World War II vet, a Navy nurse. She trained at Kings County in Brooklyn and got assigned to Bellevue in New York City.

Harry did not tell them she could read people better than anyone Harry'd ever known. But he did tell them she grew up with ten siblings in a hotel and bar in Wilkes-Barre, Pennsylvania, coal mining country, on the banks of the Susquehanna River, during the Great Depression.

DETECTIVE FIELDS had hit a wall in the Brigette Whitecloud case. He wondered if she'd show up someday dead or alive. He was toying with the idea of giving Mrs. Whitecloud the declaration she wanted. Maybe then Brigette would reappear, and the case would suddenly be solved. It would be good news - bad news. Good news, she's alive - bad news, she's going to jail for insurance fraud.

The hit and run case also stalled.

"SCHWARTZ AND WEISS, how may I direct your call?"

"Harry McHugh, please."

"Who may I say is calling?"

"Ellie Fowler."

"Thank you. One moment please."

"Hello."

"Harry, there's an Ellie Fowler for you on line 5."

"Tell her I'm out."

"Should I take a message?"

"No. Tell her I'm tied up and get her phone number."

"OK. Harry."

"Thanks, Becky."

"I'm sorry. He's meeting with a client. Can I get your phone number?"

"Meeting with a client? He's a messenger for Christ's sake. Tell him I'm at the Beverly-Wilshire. Room 1237. I don't know the telephone number."

"Hello."

"Hey, Harry. I told her you were meeting with a client and she yelled at me, said you were only a messenger for Christ's sake."

"OK."

"Harry. Don't hang up."

"What?"

"She said she's at the Beverly-Wilshire, Room 1237. She didn't have the phone number. If you'd like, Harry, I'll get it for you."

"No thanks, Becky. But thanks for the offer."

"You're welcome, Harry."

"TOBY, DID YOU ever talk to Brigette about your ethnicity?"

"Did I tell her I was Native American?"

"Yes."

"When?"

"It came up in our very first conversation."

"Really?"

"Yes. Why do you ask?"

"It finally occurred to me that Whitecloud is an Indian name. Ogallala is an Indian word, and there is an Ogallala band of Sioux Indians."

"Harry. I'm impressed. Have you been reading behind my back?"

"Yep. So, what did you two talk about?"

"When she was driving and paying attention to the road, I kept looking at her profile. She had piercing liquid black eyes and a long aquiline nose. Lips like mine. I kept thinking of my aunt who died in a car crash. My dad's favorite sister. Linda."

"Sorry to hear that."

"Anyway, I said to Brigette, 'May I ask you a question?' And I asked her what her nationality was. I told her she looked like a relative of mine."

"She said she was half Irish and half Ogallala Sioux."

"Then she asked me if I had any Indian blood."

"I told her I was half Humptulip and half Norwegian. Like almost everyone, she'd never heard of Humptulip, either."

"Is her dad still around?"

"He died when she was in high school. Leukemia."

"What did he do for a living?"

"He drove a gasoline truck. But with his other waking hours he cared for Indian ponies. When he died, his son took over the ponies with Brigette's help."

"Did she drink or do drugs?"

"No. We'd do girl's night out and go to movies, the Hollywood Bowl, the Greek, Dorothy Chandler. We saw our favorite movie together at the Nuart, in Santa Monica, 'Little Big Man.'"

"Loved that movie." Harry started imitating Dustin Hoffman's character, "'That was the end of my religion period' - 'Miss Pendrake, I am Jack Crabbe' - 'You go *down* there, General.'"

"Now do you hate the White Man, Grandfather?"

"What was she doing with a guy like Arnie?"

"What are you doing with a girl like me?"

"So, the answer is true love?"

"I don't know, Harry. But I was pretty much repelled by the guy."

"Teddy told me the bass player said the last time he saw her she was in shock."

"Really? Something very serious must have happened."

"Did you ever see any bruises on her?"

"No."

"FIELDS HERE."

"Detective, it's Peevey."

"Hi, Bill. What'd you find?"

"The Jensen car is registered. No outstanding tickets. It's clean."

"OK. Thanks, Bill."

"You're welcome, Detective."

"Wait, Bill. Who's the current owner?"

"Current owner?"

"Why it's Jensen, Detective."

"Did Beverly Hills Porsche ever take title?"

"No. It's a one-owner."

"And registration is current?"

"Yes."

"OK, thanks."

THE DAY WAS AWASH in sunshine. Martin Luther King, Jr. Elementary School teemed with visitors for the Spring Concert. Before the performance started, Harry and Toby meandered in front of the school among parents, teachers and kids, keeping an eye out for Teddy and Ella. Ella was with her kids. Teddy had taken to roaming about looking for Harry and Toby.

"Harry!"

"Hi, Teddy."

"Toby, you look beautiful."

"My Sunday Best."

"Harry, like those threads."

"Thanks," said Harry. "Geez, this place looks like the start of an Easter Parade."

"Let's go find some seats," Teddy said.

The kids were precious. The whole show tugged at Harry's heart. The looks on the parents' faces were timeless. And deep in the program an "Old Man River" solo with a humming chorus brought the crowd to its feet.

After the concert, Ella said, "My parents invited all of us for dinner, would you like to come?"

Harry and Toby took a quick look at each other and nodded.

"Follow us," Teddy said, "and stay close it's about twenty minutes."

———◆◆◆———

AT ELLA'S PARENTS' house, cooking was going on inside and out.

The men were in the backyard. Ella's dad manned the grill. Teddy and Harry hovered around him, beers in hand.

Dodger talk reigned. Everyone praised Tommy Lasorda and how far he'd taken the Dodgers in his first two years at the helm.

Harry brought up Jim Healy's Lasorda tapes. Tommy, the reporter asked, what is your opinion of Dave Kingman's performance? The tape was hilarious, Lasorda cursing a blue streak. And Healy's bleeps and sound effects made it even funnier.

The women, inside the kitchen, stood near the stove, talking about what Mrs. Williams was making. She was stirring a large pot of what she called "Chicago Beans," and keeping an eye on a cast-iron skillet with shoe-string potatoes frying in it. She coaxed Ella with the salad, so it'd be ready same time as her stuff on the stove and the ribeye outside. And, she had a lemon meringue pie waiting on the windowsill.

Everyone sat down to dinner and Mr. Williams said grace.

"Mrs. Williams," Harry exclaimed, "these are the best beans I've ever tasted. Ever!"

"They're Chicago Beans, Harry."

"I've never heard of them before. Are you from Chicago, Mrs. Williams?"

Ella, Teddy and her father quickly glanced at one and other, eyes twinkling.

"No, Harry. I'm from Westfield, Alabama. But once you eat these beans, you're gonna think you went to the Windy City."

Uproarious laughter all around.

Later, sitting in the living room over pie and coffee, Teddy updated everyone on the Whitecloud case. He gave a synopsis of his investigation and pointed out Jensen's inconsistent statements. Mrs. Williams said he lied about contact with Brigette at his house and her house, and he lied about his car.

Ella asked Toby if she thought Brigette would go into hiding for months and months.

"Only to hide out from him, if she felt she was in danger from him."

Mr. Williams said Brigette was in shock that one time, and in real fear of the rock-and-roller. "Teddy. I don't think you're the only one looking for her, unless he stopped, because he knows he doesn't have to no more."

"WHAT A GREAT DAY we had," Toby said on the way back. "I'm out first thing tomorrow morning, Harry. I have to go home. Are you going to study tonight?"

"I have to."

"It's probably better you just drop me off. I want to give my sister Mary a call and see how the family's doing."

Harry dropped Toby off at her place.

A few minutes later, Harry pulled into his driveway; and there, standing on the porch, Ellie Fowler. Harry felt like he'd dodged a bullet, dropping Toby off before going home.

"Where were you?" Ellie asked.

"What are you doing here?"

"Why didn't you call me?"

He ignored the question.

"I've got to study tonight. I'll call you a cab."

"I'm getting a divorce, Harry."

"Good for you."

"A divorce, Harry."

"I heard you."

"Harry. It's cold out here. Can we go inside."

"No. Give me a moment. I'll call the cab."

"I'm not going to beg, Harry."

"Good."

From inside, Boomer was scratching at the door and barking.

"Is that Boomer?"

"Yes."

"I love, Boomer. Let me see him, Harry."

"No."

"Then fuck you, Harry. I hope you rot in hell."

Gail had come out of her house next door and was coming down the back steps when she heard Ellie's angry outburst. Harry waved at Gail. She waved back and asked Harry if he needed anything from Ralph's Super Market.

"No thanks."

Ellie, loud enough for Gail to hear again, shrieked: "You're a loser, Harry. If you ever pass the bar, you'll never get clients and never make money."

Ellie was on a roll. Harry was thinking, *She's taken her cheerleading skills to the dark side.*

"You want me to call you a cab, or not?"

"I need to use the bathroom."

Harry didn't believe her. But he gave in to her to quell the racket and opened the door. Boomer jumped up and laid his paws on Harry's shoulders. Boomer dropped down and started sniffing Ellie. Harry didn't restrain him.

"Boomer. Hi Boomer," she said, pushing him away. Boomer made a low growl and headed toward his dog bowl.

"I'm calling a cab."

"Goddamnit, Harry."

"I'm not doing this, Ellie."

The phone rang. Harry knew it was Toby. He let it ring.

"You're new girlfriend, Harry?"

Harry went to the phone, dialed 4-1-1 and asked for the number for Yellow Cab.

"I'm not leaving, Harry."

Harry reached into a big bag on the counter for a handful of dry dog food and dropped it into Boomer's bowl.

"Look. I've got work and school tomorrow. I've got to study. I'll give you a ride to your hotel."

The phone rang again.

"You better get it, Harry."

Harry let it ring out.

"Harry, women don't like to be ignored. You should answer it."

"Let's go, Ellie."

"Harry. How 'bout a drink before we go? I'm parched. What do you have? I bet you have a beer."

Harry went to the kitchen. She freed the two top buttons on her silk blouse, stressed to their limits.

"Here. It's a Carta Blanca."

She took a sip. "It's good. Aren't you drinking?"

"No."

She nursed her beer and started talking about their years apart. She told Harry more than he wanted to hear in exceedingly explicit terms. And she wouldn't stop.

There was a knock at the door. It jarred Harry's nervous system, already on edge. *How would he explain this to Toby?* he thought. He went to the door, doomed to watch his past turn his present into ashes. Time enough had passed since the last unanswered phone call for Toby to have walked over.

He opened the door with Boomer barking wildly at his side. What a surprise. It was Ron Cohen, and from that moment on, Ron became Harry's favorite Jewish savior since Jesus Christ.

"Ron!"

"Hey, Harry. I called a couple times but no answer."

"Come on in."

"Is it safe?"

"Show no fear and Boomer'll treat you right."

"You sure, Harry?"

"Yeah, come on in."

Ron went in warily.

"So, Harry," Ron started out, not knowing Ellie sat a few feet away.

"Oh, I'm sorry, Harry. I didn't know you had company."

"Ron, this is Ellie; Ellie, Ron."

"Hi."

What a looker and what knockers, Ron thought to himself.

"I didn't mean to disturb you."

"It's OK," Harry said. "So, what's up, Ron?"

Ron spoke to Harry but stole looks at Ellie.

"I'm on my way into the office. Adam needs a Lis Pendens and Quiet Title Complaint by first thing tomorrow morning. I thought you might be able to help me out."

"Sure. I was about to take Ellie to the Beverly-Wilshire. I can be to the office a few minutes after that."

"A few minutes?" Ron said, looking to Ellie for a reaction, and knowing he could not deliver such a package to such a place for such a short time.

⁂

"PEEVEY HERE."

"Hi, Bill. Teddy Fields."

"Hi, Detective."

"How would you like some overtime?"

"Always."

"Do you have time this afternoon. I'd like to clue you in on that case involving the car I had you look into."

"Sure."

When Peevey came in, Detective Fields emphasized how Jensen lied at every turn about Brigette. Detective Fields wanted to determine Jensen's usual comings and goings, what daily life was like. Was there a pattern? Could he have her tied up inside?

Peevey asked about search warrants or wiretapping. Detective Fields told him they did not have enough to convince a judge, but Fields believed Brigette's disappearance was on Jensen.

Peevey went on to monitor the comings and goings of Jensen and the Porsche. He watched Jensen's place and had two other plain-clothesmen take up the slack.

Nobody came or went from Jensen's except pizza guys, Chinese guys, the Culligan man, the meter readers, the maids, and the pool man. No women. Jensen was a recluse. Peevey'd tail him to Ralph's or a Sunset motel. No one there matched Brigette's photo.

At one point after all the monotony, Peevey was convinced a visitor must have gone in without his noticing, because Peevey saw the suspected visitor leave. He wore a Dodger cap and dark glasses. He drove a Mercedes sport coupe. Peevey snapped a photo of it, had it developed at the station, and personally handed it to Detective Fields.

Fields took a magnifying glass to it, focusing on the face of the driver. With the glare on the windshield, the hat, glasses, steering wheel and hand on the wheel blocking the face, together with the blur from the motion of the car, it was not possible to identify the driver.

A call came into Detective Field's desk for Peevey. It was Peevey's plain-clothesman. The detective handed Peevey the phone.

"He's back. It's Jensen."

"What do you mean?"

"It was Jensen took the Mercedes. It's back in the garage."

"Thanks. Stay on it."

"Yes, Sir."

Peevey handed the phone back to Detective Fields.

"I should have known, Detective. You had me run the Mercedes but I jumped to the conclusion, he had a visitor."

Pointing to the photo, Peevey groaned, "That's Jensen."

"It's OK. Can you follow him into the grocery store and see what he's buying?"

"Sure. Anything in particular, Detective?"

"Tampax would get us a warrant."

"You think she's in there?"

"I don't know she's not."

PEEVEY'S PLAIN-CLOTHESMAN scored a hit. Jensen bought a box of Tampax at Ralph's.

Detective Fields got the DA to get a search warrant. Fields led the search. No Brigette. The new box of Tampax was in the cabana with an old, nearly empty one, near a couple dozen new bikinis. Jensen was getting ready for upcoming pool parties with the change of weather.

The cadre of police conducting the search for Detective Fields stood before him in Jensen's driveway to report they'd found nothing. Fields then had the forensic team dust the house, Porsche and Mercedes for fingerprints, and had the photographers capture every foot of the cars and the place.

BEFORE THE PHOTOS were developed and before the prints were run, Detective Fields was called into the precinct captain's office.

"How is that rock-and-roll missing-person case going?"

Detective Fields laid out the facts and progress on it.

"No more surveillance, Ted. With the search you did, you got all you could out of Jensen. She's not there. We've got a lot to do around here. It's not a good use of our resources. You know I've always had your back. You're a really good detective. You probably know your colleagues are not colorblind like I am. Don't give them any fodder to poke fun at you."

"Thanks, Captain."

"Oh. And how's that Melrose hit and run?"

"I'm going to talk to the eyewitness again."

"Good."

It didn't take long for the leers and jeers from other detectives, the mutterings when Detective Fields walked by, or the laughter behind his back.

Someone left a box of Tampax on his desk sitting on a large "Wanted Poster" showing an academy photo of a younger Officer Fields with a cowboy hat drawn on his head in magic marker. Above: "WANTED"; below: "TAMPAX TEDDY aka THE KOTEX KID"; and, in smaller print: "If you have any information contact S. Holmes at 221B Baker Street, London, England."

Detective Fields rolled up the poster, grabbed the box of Tampax, and took them home to Ella.

At home, Ella examined Teddy's haul.

"I'm shocked, Teddy. Totally shocked. I could never imagine those crackers could be that steeped in literature. Arthur Conan Doyle no less. And thanks for this," she said, holding up the box, "you saved me a trip to the store."

RON GOT THE FIRM'S Dodger tickets for a game with the Reds. He asked Harry to bring Teddy and a friend. Harry asked Teddy and his father-in-law.

Boys night out. Mr. Williams knew the players cold. He was a baseball man through and through. He'd played in the Negro Leagues after World War II.

He limited himself to one Dodger dog, one beer and one bag of peanuts. Ron, Teddy and Harry were not so disciplined.

The game was a pitching duel, Tom Seaver and Bob Welch. A couple defensive plays by Reggie Smith and Ron Cey stood out and kept the game scoreless.

Besides bouncing beach balls, the peanut vendor provided a little excitement in the stands. He stood on the aisle at one end of a row halfway up the section and threw bags of peanuts up, down, and across to hungry fans. Every throw was on the mark and most of the bags were caught. Money was passed across aisles, and off he hustled to the next section.

The peanut vendor did not have the only good arm that night. But even with no score, fans started leaving in the seventh inning. Brake lights multiplied in the parking lot.

LA fans were notorious for leaving early from Dodger Stadium. It turned out, staying put was worth it.

And Mr. Williams called it.

"If he throws Dusty a fast ball here we can pack up and go home."

"How can you tell?"

"Dusty dug in deeper than usual with his right heel. He's anchored for a long ball."

Sure enough, Dusty Baker plastered the next pitch over the left-field wall, a walk-off homer in the bottom of the 10th.

"MR. D'AMBROSIO thank you for coming in."

"Anyting I canna do to help."

"Mr. D'Ambrosio, you've been in here before?"

"Yes."

"And you told the police officer what you saw. And what happened."

"Yes."

"And do you remember questions about the car and the driver?"

"Yes. But I no really having the answers."

"What do you mean."

"I meana I seea the lady and the bambina getting hit. Ima running to them and seeing the car not astopping. I tella myself getta the license."

"I see a blonda driving but don't seea the face. I look at the license plate."

"And you remembered the numbers even when you went to work?"

"Si. I meana yes."

"And you wrote it down on a piece of paper?"

"Yes."

"Where did you put it?"

"I havea the drawer. I putta the recipe. The receipt. The invoice. Pens. Paper. Junk."

"And you searched it thoroughly?"

"Many, many times."

"What do you think happened to it?"

"I think it falla behind or falla out. I looked and looked. Maybe it getta swept up somatime."

"So you think it's gone."

"Afraid it is."

"But you remembered some of the letters and some of the numbers?"

"Yes. I tella the cops."

"Do you remember, right now today what the letters and numbers were?"

"Oh. I notta think about it since I talka to the cops."

"Can you give me your best recollection?"

He sighed and took a deep breath.

"OK. "M" – "Z" – "L" and "5" maybe "9"."

"Thank you. Now, what kind of car was it?"

"Foreign."

"Do you remember what you told the police?"

"I tella them I'm notta sure. It's a grey like a silver. That's why they bringa me to the station."

"Did you look through pictures of cars?"

"Yes."

"You picked one out, right?"

"Right."

"Were you sure that was the right car?"

"No. I'm notta sure."

"Did you tell the officer you weren't sure."

"Yes."

"OK. Let me show you the pictures again? All right?"

"Sure."

Chef D'Ambrosio was overwhelmed and confused with all the cars and models. Truth was, like he said, he'd zeroed in on the license plate only.

"Mr. D'Ambrosio what kind of car do you have?"

"I don't havea one."

"Did you ever drive?"

"Oh, yes. But I was in accident and got a concussion. Sometimes I black out. I saw a doctor and doctor tella me notta to drive."

"I see. Just do your best. Take your time. I'll be back."

When Detective Fields returned, Mr. D'Ambrosio had three pictures out, all 1976 models: a BMW 3.0, a BMW 2500, and a Mercedes 450 SL. His prior selection was the BMW 2500.

Detective Fields looked at the photos and literally froze.

"Just a minute," he said.

He walked to a file cabinet and pulled out a file. He took it to his desk and opened it on top of the car pictures already covering the top of the desk. He thumbed through the folder and pulled out Jensen photos. There it was. A 450 SL, license number MZL 953. Detective Fields turned the photo for Mr. D'Ambrosio to see.

"Thatsa the one."

"Mr. D'Ambrosio, you like a ride home?"

"Yes. But no uza the siren. I gotta dog at home. She hatesa the siren."

"Don't worry. No sirens."

"HELLO."

"Harry?"

"Teddy?"

The Melrose hit and run eyewitness just ID'd Jensen's car."

"What?"

"The license plate matches. And I've been looking at photos of Jensen's car for weeks. But I never put two and two together."

"What does this mean for Brigette?"

"Think about it, Harry. She and Jensen came back to Jensen's in early August. She was in shock and afraid of Jensen. They gave her four Vicodin. You saw her a couple weeks later. She was likely in the car with him. The hit and run driver was a blonde. Long-haired Jensen.

"We arrest Jensen. Ask the public again for additional witnesses. All that should smoke Brigette out of hiding, if she's alive. If she doesn't come out, or if we can't prove damage to the car, then the case hinges on our eyewitness. As to Brigette, we'll still need a body."

FINALS WERE COMING UP. The study group was making good progress. Miguel got hold of old bar exam essay questions and multi-state exams. And between those items, Gilbert Law Summaries and Canned Briefs, there was no end to exam-prep material.

Harry boiled things down to basics in Evidence. Penny made a list of potential issues in Real Property. And Carol followed suit in Corporations. They were looking at three different subjects with little overlap between them.

In the end, Miguel got the best grades of the group, likely because he gave each subject the same amount of attention. Harry, Carol and Penny got the highest grades in their individual focus subjects, but not the others.

AFTER FINALS, HARRY had the study group over for a barbecue.

Penny brought her latest boyfriend, a DA from downtown, and her daughter, who loved Boomer. Carol came with her twin sister. Miguel showed up with a Spanish professor from East Los Angeles College. Harry asked Gail, Pepper and Sean from next door, the Toledanos from across the street, and Ron and Becky from work. Teddy and Ella came with Ella's mom and dad.

Toby was flying but expected back about halfway through the party. After changing out of her stewardess uniform, she walked over to Harry's. She could hear the party from down the street. Everyone was yelling and laughing in the middle of a charades game. Toby knocked on the screen door and Boomer bounded toward it. Becky jumped up to let her in.

Finally, Harry's girlfriend, unveiled to his closest friends. He had kept her under wraps for months. Her entrance halted the charades game.

Penny could not believe her eyes. Harry had thrown her curves before but nothing like Toby's. Becky liked Toby from the moment she opened the door and they smiled at each other. Ron muttered to himself, *how* does *he do it*. Gail could tell right away Harry'd traded way up from that bitch on his porch. Pepper was happy for Harry.

Harry put a plate together for Toby, piled high with all the fixings. She sat at the kitchen table with Ella and shared the plate with Boomer. Sean came through for a Coke and Ella asked him if he wanted another plate.

"No, thanks. Four's plenty. It was great."

"What grade are you in Sean?"

"Sophomore."

"What high school?"

"Fairfax."

"Do you have plans for college?"

"Yes, Ma'am."

"Where?"

"Depends on baseball."

"Baseball?"

"I'm hoping for a scholarship."

"Wait a second. I'll be right back."

Ella returned with an autographed baseball card and handed it to Sean.

"Whoa. Willie Mays!"

"Yep."

Sean was beaming.

Teddy stuck his head in the kitchen.

"I'm sorry, babe, but it's time to make tracks."

"Oh. Toby just got here."

"I know. But we've got a long drive and your folks are passed their bedtime."

"I think they're having fun. See if they can last a little longer."

"Sure."

MONTHS LATER, HARRY got Becky to tamper with his schedule. He wanted to attend Jensen's trial. Jensen got Benjamin Shapiro to represent him. He demanded a jury trial. Shapiro prepped Jensen six ways from Sunday. He was ready to take the stand, even though he didn't have to.

Shapiro planned on shredding the eyewitness over the license plate number. But whether he cracked, or not, Shapiro'd put Jensen's fame and facile mendacity to work to seal the deal.

The judge displayed a special deference toward Shapiro. Maybe because Shapiro's office had donated thousands to the judge's recent re-election campaign.

In any event, Jensen showed up in a navy blazer, white shirt, striped tie, grey dress pants, shiny cordovan loafers, and not quite a military haircut -- a polite preppy look.

The jury was mixed-race, two more women than men, and a couple of them barely spoke English.

Harry knew to get in line at the courthouse early to make it into the gallery. It was a bit of a media circus.

Shapiro commanded the courtroom from the start.

"Why in all my years I cannot remember dealing with a case where the police wanted so much to charge some person, any person, even if it was the wrong person. This case turns on one witness and one witness only. No one else has come forward against my client. And that one witness cannot even identify my client.

"The witness admits he never saw the driver's face.

"Let's get this straight right now. A terrible tragedy occurred. Someone ran down a young mother and her three-year old child. It was horrific. And whoever did it never stopped the car but barreled on away from the scene of the accident as fast as could be.

"This is a case, one like no other. I have never seen such a case where there is no physical evidence. Nothing about a dented bumper or scraped paint or anything to do with the car itself.

"Look. It's natural when something this awful happens, to be angered by it, and to want to make someone pay for it. But the state here, the prosecution, has an enormous burden it cannot meet, to prove its case beyond a reasonable doubt. Beyond a reasonable doubt, ladies and gentlemen. The evidence here is not enough. It's not enough. My client is innocent."

Harry noticed a man across the aisle agonizing over every word, wincing when the victims were mentioned. Harry approached the man at the break.

"Excuse me," Harry said to him, "do you know the victims?"

The question jolted the man.

"I'm sorry," Harry said, "I want you to know I was deputized by LAPD to investigate Jensen. I worked on this case."

"My sister and niece." He could barely speak.

"I'm really sorry."

The bailiff re-opened the doors, and Harry and the man went in and sat down next to each other. Harry offered his hand and said his name. The man took his hand and whispered, "Bill Gonzales."

They talked some more during the day and spent the rest of trial shoulder to shoulder. Bill asked Harry one legal question after another, when he learned Harry was studying law, to explain what was going on, and what effect it was having on the jury.

The eyewitness was the head chef from Chianti. He testified he got off the bus and was on his way to work walking on Melrose Avenue when up ahead he saw the mother and child step into the crosswalk at Fuller when the light went red on Melrose, green on Fuller.

They took a few steps and a car hit them. They were thrown into the air and landed like rag dolls on the pavement ahead. He remembered hearing a thud and a woman's scream. The prosecutor asked if he heard screeching tires. Shapiro objected, leading. "No screeching tires," the witnessed testified, before the objection was sustained. And the witness added, "The car never slowed down. It sped up. The mother never let go of the baby's hand."

Shapiro let it go. The chef went on that, the car barreled past him, and he saw the license plate.

Bill Gonzales was fighting back tears throughout the testimony.

The chef raced to the stricken mother and child and saw blood pouring from their skulls. His gory description fit the crime-scene photos the prosecutor showed on several poster boards mounted on easels directly across from the jurors.

The chef testified he kept repeating the license plate number to himself and wrote it down, but admittedly, later lost it. He could not identify the driver and Shapiro got him to say he thought it was a woman with blonde hair. He was not sure of the make and model of the car, either. In closing argument, Shapiro pointed to these facts as overwhelming evidence, sufficient to cast reasonable doubt on the prosecution's case.

When Shapiro took him on, it went in part like this: "You focused on the license plate, you don't know what the driver looked like, or if there were passengers or not, correct?"

"Correct."

"But whatever the license number was you cannot remember today?"

"No. Not today."

"And even though you wrote it down before, you don't have that piece of paper now?"

"No."

"And, in fact, you never saw that paper again, after you put it in your junk drawer?"

"Right."

"And the police helped you pick out a car from photographs, right?"

"Yes."

In his closing argument, Shapiro reminded the jury of something they'd never heard before. He told them when a person witnesses a traumatic event, blood and guts as it were, it is not unusual to block out or forget the sequence of events. It would be gratuitous expertise on Shapiro's part to go beyond all evidence in the case, but he did, and he knew the DA would object to it in a way that would draw even more attention to the remarks and elevate them in the minds of jurors.

It was Shapiro, working his own kind of black magic. And Shapiro also knew the judge would deny the DA's objection, and indeed he did, giving even more credence to Shapiro's made-up traumatized-witness theory.

Shapiro trusted his own instincts more than any book on trial strategy, even the three he had written himself.

He knew the most truthful witnesses could get tripped up and show a lack of credibility. People, as honest as can be, like Chianti's chef, can unravel before a wily attorney and a staring jury.

And maybe more important, Shapiro knew he had a great witness in Jensen. Shapiro had spent hours with him. Shapiro knew Jensen could stick to a story. He knew he could not be rattled. He knew Jensen was a born liar.

But the jury didn't.

Harry was appalled at the outcome. He second-guessed his career choice. He wanted to be a great lawyer one day. But maybe being a great lawyer was different than retiring from the legal profession with a conscience intact.

After the verdict was read by the clerk, and the courtroom emptied out, Harry asked Bill if he wanted to go somewhere and talk about it.

"No thanks, Harry. I'm sorry. I gotta go home."

DETECTIVE FIELDS LEARNED of the verdict from a call from the bailiff immediately after it was read. Detective Fields asked the bailiff to grab Harry and have him call him.

Harry and Teddy agreed to meet at Molly Malone's on Fairfax north of 6th Street. The place was dark and smelled like a beer cellar. Dimly lit paintings of Irish poets, writers, heroes of the rebellion and JFK adorned the walls above wooden booths to the left. A long mahogany bar to the right had rows of liquors and a mirror behind it. A jukebox featured Irish tunes, and a banner advertised Live Music from Irish Folksingers on Friday and Saturday nights.

Half the crowd at Molly's on any given night had left the old sod and overstayed their visas in the US. A good majority of them were either looking for the perfect American spouse, plotting a fake marriage for a green card, or awaiting an IRA assignment.

Harry got there first, took a booth, and started with Jameson's on the rocks. Teddy showed up and asked Harry what to drink.

"It's all good. They have Guinness beer, Jameson's, Bushmills, Irish Coffee, Bailey's and anything else not-Irish you might like. It's a full bar.

"When in Rome," Teddy said, "I'll have what you're having."

"Jameson's on the rocks. It's Irish whiskey."

"A day like today calls for it. Doesn't it?"

"Mm-hmm."

Harry popped out of the booth, the waitress didn't start 'til later, and leaned on the bar.

"Two more, please," he said, pushing his empty glass toward the bartender.

Harry returned to the booth with the drinks.

"Cheers," they said, clinking their glasses together."

"But nothing to cheer about," Harry said.

"No. What was it? What got him off?"

"Shapiro had them totally confused about reasonable doubt. There was no damage to the car or repair evidence. Jensen lied liked a rug and they bought it. And, of course, no Brigette."

"Lawyers."

"You got that right, Teddy. Jensen walks."

"We needed Brigette. Now she might suddenly appear. She doesn't have to worry about Jensen. He's in the clear. Harry, how did the victim's brother take it?"

"Complete and utter despair. He walked away sickened."

"Do you think he might go after Jensen?"

"No. Not in any physical way. He's wants me to file a civil action for him."

"Your first client, Harry."

"If I pass the bar."

Looking around Molly Malone's, Teddy asked Harry if he came there much.

"No. A few times. First time I came was with my study group. It was a Saturday night. We sang along with the band. Nobody knew the words. But a lot of the Irish songs have repetitive refrains. We not only started nailing them, but with all the drink that night, even Miguel started sounding like a Mick.

"It was the first time in my life I'd had Irish coffee. I never drink coffee. I think I had six or seven of them that night. I finally crawled into bed around 2:30 a.m., drunk as a skunk, and laid there, eyes wide open, ears still ringing, until dawn. The coffee kept me up."

"You know any Irish jokes, Harry, to cheer us up?"

"One. Mr. Guinness, himself, the owner of the Guinness Brewery in Dublin marched down to Tom O'Shaunessy's wee, humble cottage only yards from the banks of the River Liffey. Mr. Guinness stood in the doorway. 'Katie,' he said in a consoling voice, 'I've got bad news for you, your Tommy fell into the big vat and drowned.'

"'Ach,' she cried, 'not the big vat, oh my poor Tommy, he never had a chance!'

"'Well, Katie, I'm not so sure about that. You see, he got out three times to take a pee.'"

Teddy roared.

Harry was feeling the whiskey now.

"Teddy, do you know what Irish foreplay is?"

"No. What?"

"Three little words, 'Brace yourself, Maggie!' Look. One more joke and I'll shut up."

"Keep 'm coming, Harry. You're on a roll," Teddy said, finishing off his Jameson's with a quick double-shake of his head.

"This is not an Irish joke, but it is indirectly, in the sense it mocks the British."

"Go ahead."

"Did you hear about the Frenchman who stood before the judge for necrophilia?"

"No."

"You know what necrophilia is?"

"Harry, I'm a Hollywood police detective. Having sex with a corpse."

"The judge asked the Frenchman if he had anything to say in his own defense for what he did."

In Harry's best French accent, he said, "'I do your honor. I did not know she was dead. I thought she was English.'"

After a second's pause Teddy let out a big laugh.

They had a few more drinks. Harry asked Teddy how he ended up on the force. Teddy told him he grew up in a big family in Washington, DC. His dad drove a bus, his mom was a teacher's aide. Teddy was all-city in basketball and got a scholarship to the University of San Francisco, graduated, and went to Vietnam. He was an MP officer in Saigon, came back, moved in with a cousin in Compton, and made it into the police academy.

"Basketball? Aren't you about 5'10"?"

"Yep. But ten years ago, I could dunk."

"And now?"

"And now, like any other cop, I'm still dunkin' -- donuts."

"MOM!"

"Brigette!"

"Sorry, I couldn't call you."

"Where are you? What happened?"

"I'm in LA. I've been safe. But I was a passenger in a hit and run where a mother and child were killed. The driver is a famous singer and he told me he'd kill me if I said anything. And I believed him. They finally found him. He went to trial but got off."

"Did you testify?"

"No. I was hiding out."

"Why didn't you turn him in? Make an anonymous call to the police?"

"He had me terrified. He kidnapped me for several days. Told me he'd kill me if I said anything. I feel awful for the victims. I don't know how he could have gotten off at trial, but he did. Now I feel worse for not testifying."

"Oh, Brigette. I'm so glad to hear from you. Where have you been, what have you been doing?"

"I've been working with horses. Giving rides in the Santa Monica mountains."

"Your dad'd be happy for you. Oh, I'm so glad you're all right. I want you to call Detective Fields, LAPD. He sounds like a good man. Will you do that for me?"

"Sure, Mom. How are you? How is Nick?"

"We're fine. Now that I hear from you, we're better than fine. Do you want the detective's number?"

"Yes."

"Talk to him, then call me back."

EMPLOYEE REVIEWS took place at Schwartz & Weiss in the beginning of December. Bonuses were handed out the day before the Christmas holiday. Harry was one of the last employees to get his yearly review.

Ron called the library and Harry picked up.

"How'd you do on your review, Harry?"

"I did OK. How 'bout you?"

"Let's save it for the The Pub. You available after work?"

"Sure."

For a Tuesday night, The Pub was packed. The Laker-Celtic game, televised from Boston, had drawn the crowd.

"You want to catch dinner instead?" Ron asked.

"Sure. Where?"

"This way." Ron started toward the up-escalator leading to street level.

"Kurotoshuro or the Playboy Club. You're call. They're both walking distance."

"I'm thinking Sushi, tempura, teriyaki, and Kirin beer before I picture a bunny tail and the swooping delivery of drinks to the table."

"Harry, I thought you'd jump at the Playboy Club."

"Nah."

"Harry, your hopeless. All your girlfriends could do justice to the bunny outfit. I'm a mere mortal."

Harry laughed. "OK. Let's go to the Club."

"No. I need some quiet to fill you in. Anyway, I'd hate to bump into Adam or any of the others there."

"Adam's a member?"

"He always takes his clients there."

"The old horn dog."

"You don't know the half of it. Becky confided in me one day about a joke he told her. She asked me if I'd tell Adam to back off. Stupid me. I told him. He wasn't happy about it."

"What was the joke?"

"Do you know what the two biggest lies in the world are?"

"Say no more."

Kurotoshuro was a black and white modern décor Japanese restaurant. It sat across a wide mall from the Playboy Club between the Shubert Theater and Century Hotel on one side and twin forty-story triangle-shaped skyscraper office buildings on the other.

This was the heart of Century City where Harry had answered an LA Times ad for a messenger job to get him through law school, and where Ron had left a post with the governor, to come to.

When they sat down, Ron told Harry his review couldn't have gone worse, the partners were disappointed in him, they thought he'd have contributed a lot more to the firm and used his government connections for new business. They'd expected him to be a rainmaker. Bring in clients. They also told him his litigation skills were not as good as some paralegals.

"And I'm blaming you for that one, Harry, you!" Ron said, smiling and pointing a finger in Harry's face. Ron went on, "They didn't fire me, Harry. But they took me behind the woodshed."

"I'm sorry to hear that, Ron. What are you going to do?"

"I'm going to hang in, try to do better, make some phone calls to some Sacramento cronies and, if I have to, hire a headhunter."

"I'm really sorry about this."

"Harry, I'm curious. Whatever happened to Ellie."

"Ellie?"

"Yeah."

"I don't know. She may have gone back to her husband. I haven't heard anything from her."

"'Casablanca,' Harry."

"Hmm?"

"'How extravagant you are. Throwing away women like that. Some day they may be scarce.'"

"You're quoting the movies again, Ron. Claude Rains, Inspector Renault. You should go into entertainment law."

"Harry. I always had the feeling I could develop into a solid trial lawyer. Trials are where it's at for me. I went into law, not to draft contracts between studios and actors. I love movies because they gave me Clarence Darrow and Atticus Finch. And TV, because it gave me Perry Mason. I became a lawyer to do trials."

"You're right. I have no doubt you can do it. And exceedingly well. You just need to pick up the necessary skills."

"Thanks, Harry."

"HARRY, IT'S TEDDY. Doing anything tomorrow?

"Work, studying for finals, why?"

"You like seafood?"

"Love it."

"Ever been to Gladstones 4 Fish?"

"Once. It was great. Loved the view. But the prices kept me from going back."

"What if LAPD pays?"

"Sounds good. What's up?"

"You'll see."

"What time?"

"Two-thirty?"

"You got it."

GLADSTONES WAS RIGHT on the beach. It stood beyond Sunset Boulevard where it ended at Pacific Coast Highway.

When Harry got there, it had to have been high tide. The day was dark with low clouds. The surf was up, crashing only yards from the restaurant. Walking up, Harry got sprayed with ocean mist. He felt the cold, salt air, and heard the roar of the ocean and the cawing of seagulls.

Inside, Harry saw Teddy at the back of the restaurant with a woman in a booth next to a window facing the ocean. Her back was to Harry. Teddy slid over in the booth, making a place for Harry.

"Hi, Harry," she said.

"Hi, Cleo. I hope you're OK."

"I am."

"Glad to hear it."

"I'm sorry to have put you through all this."

"I can't be mad at you, Brigette. You gave me Toby."

"Detective Fields was telling me."

"What happened that first time I saw you?"

"Arnie dropped me off. I thought he was leaving. But I saw him park the car from my apartment. I ran down to the garage and hid for a moment then ran outside and saw you."

"What about that scream?"

"Coincidence, Harry. I'd asked Ivan, the apartment manager, to fix my shower. Sure enough, he let himself in with his manager's key that morning when I was out. I opened the door to the apartment and that crazy Cossack burst out of the bathroom. I was so on edge from Jensen, I thought I was a goner. I screamed bloody murder, but when I saw it was Ivan, I shooed him away and told him to come back the next day."

The waitress arrived at the table. They ordered clam chowder and fish and chips.

"After the accident, several days after, I knew I had to get away from Arnie. He'd already kidnapped me at his place, given me Vicodin and who knows what else. He threatened to kill me if I said anything. And I believed him.

"I finally convinced him I had to go back to work or they'd report me missing and the police would come straight to his place looking for me. I told him everyone at work knew I was dating him. I assured him I had his back, and I knew I needed to show him our relationship hadn't soured. So, I went along with things. He drove me home and told me to meet him at the Vagabond Motel in two days, come as a stewardess. I went there with a knife in my purse. I didn't use it. Next morning, when he got blocked in behind the garbage truck in front of your house, I told him I'd see him soon, and hopped out of the car. I didn't expect him to follow me up to my apartment.

"After I saw you, I dropped off the stewardess uniform at Western Costume and headed to Topanga Canyon to look for a job with a riding stable. I told them I'd just come from Nebraska and my dad, a full-blooded Sioux Indian, who'd spent his life tending horses, taught me everything he knew. I offered to work for room and board. They said, 'OK' and let me keep the tips from the tours I gave. It's been like that ever since."

"Did you know about the trial?"

"Yes. I didn't think he'd get off. I'm sick about not turning him in or testifying. I read that the woman he killed had no husband, no parents, no other children. I didn't think he'd get off."

"Where do you work?"

"Mountain Trails Horseback Tours in Topanga Canyon."

"So, you've been working only a few miles from here the whole time?"

"Yes."

The soup arrived.

"What's the plan?" Harry asked.

Teddy spoke up.

"The district attorney is waiting on me. He wants to interview Brigette. Jensen has double jeopardy on his side. He can't be tried twice for the same crime, hit and run.

But Brigette has civil and criminal claims against him, unrelated to his double-jeopardy defense. He drugged her and wouldn't let her go for days after the hit and run. You know what that means, Harry?"

"Mm-hmm. The DA has a solid case for kidnapping, assault and battery, and you'll get the collar, Teddy. The civil claims overlap -- false imprisonment, assault and battery, plus intentional infliction of emotional distress. Any one of these intentional torts gives rise to punitive damages."

Brigette spoke up. "Harry. I want him to pay. But I want it to go to the woman's family. Like a nearest relative if she has one. She must have extended family of some kind. I'd want them to get the money, not me."

"Brigette. She has a brother. A real good guy. He's got a wife and kids. He's a machinist."

"OK."

"But that's not all. You have your action, for what I just described, and the brother has his own, for wrongful death. In other words, there could be two separate civil lawsuits against Jensen."

"And" Teddy added, "the DA can charge him criminally and put him behind bars for what he did to you."

"Look, Harry. I want you to take my case."

"I'm not an attorney yet, and won't be, for at least a year. But your case'll take a couple years to get to trial," Harry paused for a moment wishing Ron and Miguel were there to hear his next line, "unless he makes you an offer you can't refuse."

"Could you work on the case, Harry, until you pass the bar, and take it over?"

"Sure. My firm has an attorney in it, I could steer the case to him. He's not a partner, but he'll stand up for you, and he has a heart of gold."

THE END